1

CHOSEN

ANNALIESE LAYAW

Bible quotes from (NASB2020)(ESV)(NIV)

TABLE OF CONTENTS

"BUT YOU ARE A CHOSEN PEOPLE, A ROYAL PRIESTHOOD, A HOLY NATION, GOD'S SPECIAL POSSESSION, THAT YOU MAY DECLARE THE PRAISES OF HIM WHO CALLED YOU OUT OF THE DARKNESS INTO HIS WONDERFUL LIGHT."

1 PETER 2:9

For Josiah Joy,

Though your life was cut short, you continue to live in our hearts

CHAPTER ONE

The Rembricks have always been devout believers in God Almighty. Otherwise known as Christians or Christ followers. We consider the Bible to be the sole and absolute truth. That's unusual, though, for Midas, one of the many dome cities found within what's left of the United States. And in Midas, the only thing that glitters is gold. Like its namesake, the mythological king, Midas values only money and power. We believe otherwise. The problem is we are the only people in Midas who don't believe that. Just four people in a city of one million. Despite this, we've faced little opposition. It's no surprise when people give me strange looks and call me names such as "Goody-two-shoes" and "The Saint" because I'm different; I don't conform to their style of dress, I've never had a boyfriend, I don't follow trends, and I rarely say yes to anything. It used to hurt, but as I've gotten older, I've gotten used to it. But what happens when the earthquake comes? And the foundation that was holding you up falls right out from under you. And you're dangling on a cliff between certain death and a life with everything thought you wanted.

"Wanna come to my place tonight? We can do our homework and watch a movie afterward?" My dearest friend, Jenn Dillon, asked after our last class of the day. I took my books from my locker and put them in my bag. "Which movie?" "*Beneath The Vicious Skin*." I sighed. "Sorry, I can't watch that." She rolled her eyes but refused to back down. "*Electric Hearts* then?" I smiled and nodded. "That should be fine. I'll ask my parents when I get home, but there shouldn't be a problem. I'll call as soon as I know." She smiled. "Alright! Hope to see you then!" She walked away. Her dark brown ponytail bounced from side to side as she walked down the hall. I felt a tap on my shoulder. "Ready to go, Elnora?" I turned to my older brother, who had just finished his last class. I nodded. "Yep!" He waved to his friends, and we walked out. The after-school crowd surged through the streets. I stepped closer to my brother and grabbed his hand. I hate crowds. They've always made me feel uneasy. But Matthew has always been my protector. I've always known that whenever I'm nervous or afraid, he will be there.

Matthew is the best brother ever! Just a year older than me, we've been best friends since we were little. He's always been my guardian and confidante. With a well-styled mop of brown curly hair and dark blue eyes, he looks just like our dad. The only difference is he's slightly taller. He's very handsome. At least, from what I can tell by how the girls at school sigh and swoon over him, always trying to get his attention. But Matthew has never had a girlfriend, nor wanted one. He just tunes out the giggly girls.

14

"How was school?" he asked me, as we settled on the train. I nodded. "It was good. Mr. Tawnwell was in a sour mood today, so science was pretty interesting," I said with a smile. "How about you?" He shrugged. "It was pretty good. There was a new guy today. His family just moved here from Ring One." My jaw dropped. "They're from Ring One? Who would move here from the center?" "He said his parents' jobs just got moved here, and the two-hour commute just wasn't worth it to them." "That makes sense." "His name is Anthony. He has two sisters, one older, one younger." "Where in the ring have they moved? Are they close by?" "I don't know. I didn't ask." "Well, if they live nearby, I'm sure Mom'll want to invite them over." "Yeah. That would be cool." I looked around the subway. A smartly dressed woman sat across the aisle from us with two little kids. Both sucked on rock candy. The woman looked worn out but was trying to keep it together. When she noticed me, she smiled. I returned the smile. An elderly man with a newspaper sat a few seats away from her. The headline read, "Rembrick Building Co. Soars". No doubt referring to the airport my parents' company had just finished building. It was only the second in Midas, but civilians never left the city. The only people who left were pilots or military. We were thousands of miles from the nearest city, so most of our resources came from very far away, making a second airport necessary. The train slowed as the conductor announced the next stop.

We got off at Station Axwell, and walked down Axwell Street to Corman, then down our street, Cassio

15

Lane. Ring Three houses uniformly match ours: small, white, simple, modest fenced yards, and tiny front porches barely big enough for three people. We stepped inside and the smell of whatever wonder that Mom was making for dinner greeted us like a warm hug. "Hey Mom! We're home," I called to her. "Hey, kiddos! How was school?" "It was good," I told her as we walked into the kitchen. "Good! Go put your bags in your rooms. Dinner will be ready in just a few minutes." Matthew started upstairs, but I walked over to her next to the stove and hugged her. "How was work, Mom?" She smiled. "Miss Poorin still thinks she can turn Dad's head, even though I've warned her she'll be fired for it, but other than that, it was great." I laughed. "Good! That lady's got guts. Good job dealing with it with patience and grace." "Thanks, sweetie!" Still, I lingered. "Uh, Jenn asked if I could come over tonight after dinner to do homework. We'd watch a movie afterward. Do you think it would be okay?" "Which movie?" "*Electric Hearts*." "That's fine. It's a Friday, so someone will be by at ten to pick you up." I hugged her tightly. "Thanks, Mom!" She laughed. "No problem, Elnora."

"I went to visit our new neighbors," Mom said after Dad prayed for the food. "They're from Ring One, but their jobs were just moved here. They have three kids: Madison, Anthony, and Serah. Madison still lives in Ring One because she works there but stays with them on weekends. Anthony is Matthew's age, and Serah is fourteen. She's in eighth grade, so she'll be starting at the middle school on Monday. She said

Anthony started today–to get a feel for the schedule before Monday." "That's smart," Matthew commented. "I think so, too," Mom replied. "I think I met Anthony today. What's their last name?" "Merrick." "I did then. That's funny. He seems pretty cool. I saw him sitting by himself at lunch, so I sat with him." "That's great, Matthew," Dad said, nudging his son with his elbow. "Way to be a light." "Thanks." Now, it was my turn. "I'm going over to Jenn's after dinner," I told Dad. "Oh, cool! What are you going to do?" "We're going to do our homework, then watch a movie." "That sounds fun. Just make sure you get your homework done before you watch the movie. You don't want to be doing homework over the weekend." "I will. Though I don't know how much Jenn will actually want to do. I think it was just an excuse to hang out," I said with a chuckle. They all laughed. Then Dad cleared his throat and said, "Remember tomorrow's Saturday. Make sure you all have a list of what you want to do tomorrow." "I also invited the Merricks over for dinner. So, make sure you're clean and crisp by five," Mom added. "Do you think the girls would like it if I made them some welcome gifts?" I asked. "That's a wonderful idea, Elnora," Mom answered. "You should do that. I know when my family moved here from Ring Two, I would've felt so welcome if a girl my age had done that for me." "I'll do that then. I'll go to the Ring Two Shopping Centre tomorrow as well to get some things for them."

The next morning, I got up early, dressed in overalls and an old green t-shirt, then put my auburn hair in a ponytail. I quickly made myself some eggs and toast and scarfed them down. Dad and Matthew had just come downstairs by the time I had finished my breakfast. Mom had gone early to go to Ring Six to help the poor and broken people who lived there. I grabbed my small black duffel bag, tossed it over my shoulder, and left. I walked about a block to the house of an elderly widow I often helped and knocked on the door. "Good morning, Elnora," she greeted me cheerfully. "Good morning, Mrs. Comstock! I was wondering if I could weed your garden for you and mow your lawn?" She smiled brightly. "That would be delightful! I'll pay you for it. How much?" I shook my head and laughed. "Nothing at all, ma'am. It's just my way of giving back." "Oh, my goodness! What a lovely gesture! That's so kind of you!" "Of course! It's no problem! If you'll just show me where your gardening tools are, I'll get started right now."

It took about two hours to weed her front garden and mow her front and back yards. She handed me a glass of fresh lemonade before I moved on. The cool, sweet drink was refreshing after all the hard work. I went to the Ring Two Shopping Centre and found some goodies for the Merrick girls. A glass bead bracelet for each, along with cute notebooks, matching pens, and a tiny succulent. I tucked everything into gift bags and dropped them off in my room before I headed to a small family's house to offer a few hours of babysitting.

I returned home around 4:30, with half an hour to prepare for the Merricks. Mom had already returned home and had dinner well underway, of course. I changed into a crisp white V-neck T-shirt and jeans. I put together the gift bags for the girls and came back downstairs. It was 4:50. "Oh great! You're here," Mom said. "Can you set the table for me, please?" "Yes, ma'am."

I took the stack of plates from the cupboard and set them out, followed by silverware and glasses. "What should I set out for drinks?" "Get a pitcher of water with ice. Then there is a bottle of soda in the fridge that I just got from the store, and get out a bottle of fizzy cider too. That should be fine." I nodded and took the bottle of soda from the fridge, my mind already moving to what came next. I put it on the table, then got a bottle of fizzy cider from the large cabinet where we kept it. Matthew came down just as someone knocked on the door. Mom turned toward the sound. "Matthew, would you get that?" He hurried out of the room and down the hall. "Where's Dad?" I asked. "He'll be back soon. He got caught up in something right before he came home." I put a couple of scoops of ice from the freezer into the glass pitcher and filled it with water, then put it on the table.

Matthew led our guests into the kitchen. "Well, I'd offer a tour, except you won't be seeing anything new," Matthew told them with a chuckle. Mom washed her hands and wiped them on her black apron. "Hello, everyone!" She shook hands with a woman who looked to be middle-aged. "Good to see you again, Alice!" "You as well, Luci." She shook the man's hand. "Hi, I'm Luci Rembrick. My husband will be home soon. Then you can get some good man talk," she said with a laugh. "Nice to meet you, Luci. I'm Greg. It smells wonderful in here." Luci laughed. "Thank you! I have a chicken roasting, mashed potatoes, and some sauteed veggies." "Oh my! You didn't have to cook for us," Mrs. Merrick exclaimed. "Nonsense," Mom said. "I love cooking! This is a normal dinner for us." She turned to me. "This is my daughter, Elnora. And you just met Matthew." Mrs. Merrick's smile curled without warmth. Her eyes scanned me-not curious, not kind. Just measuring. I offered my hand, steady despite the chill. What was it about me she didn't like? "Nice to meet you." She acted like she hadn't heard me. "Matthew is seventeen and Elnora is sixteen." Mrs. Merrick smiled brightly as she gestured to her three teenagers. "These are our three: Madison, Anthony, and Serah." Madison had dark brown curly hair and icy blue eyes. She wore a black tank top, black pants, and black flats. She smiled confidently and extended her hand to me. I shook it. "Nice to meet you, Madison!" The boy introduced himself next. He had dark brown hair, the same as Madison's, but somehow it seemed richer, and dark brown eyes that looked like melted chocolate. He was taller than Matthew, with a steadier build. Something in me flinched-then fluttered. "Nice to meet you, Nora." *Elnora*," Matthew corrected him. I stuttered. "It's fine. Nora's fine. Some people call me that sometimes." I gave Matthew a look—soft, but wary. I'd never liked it when people called me that, but

20

now wasn't the time. Anthony smiled, and my stomach did a flip. "My turn, Anthony!" The youngest shoved him out of the way. "I'm Serah!" I laughed-not just at Serah's boldness, but at how easily she cracked the tension. She had short, straight, blonde hair, and her eyes were the same chocolate brown as Anthony's. "Anthony is a total lame-o. He's never had a girlfriend for longer than two weeks. He's a hunk, but totally dumb and boring. I would stay far away from him if I were you." "Did I miss dinner?" Dad's voice called from the door. "Hey, Honey! Come on in!" Dad walked into the kitchen. A backpack was slung over his shoulder. "What a party!" He exclaimed. He shook Mr. Merrick's hand. "Hey there, I'm Lucas. Nice to meet you." He hugged Mom and kissed her forehead. "Alright, no sense in waiting. Let's eat," Dad said.

It was a great time. Serah was all energy and opinions. Though many of the words she said I would never dare say. Madison kept mostly to herself except to try to get Matthew's attention, who didn't seem to notice at all. And Anthony-he was something else. Kind, funny, and courteous, and I've already mentioned what he did to my insides. Mrs. Merrick was a hairdresser-groomed, glamorous, and just as hollow as the girls in my year. Her gaze skimmed over me like etiquette-polite, detached, and entirely uninterested. Mr. Merrick was the head tailor for *Enchante* Co. The label adored by every woman in Rings One and Two, and envied by the richest in Ring Three. Mom invited them to dinner on Thursday. I'd hoped our families might become friends. I'd hoped I'd see Anthony again in the hallway, maybe even sit with him and Matthew at lunch. But Thursday's dinner never came. And Matthew and I never returned to school.

CHAPTER TWO

I shuffled down the stairs the next morning. Matthew sat at the table, reading his Bible. "Hey." "Hey." I grabbed cereal, milk, a bowl, and a spoon without thinking, muscle memory steering me to the table. "Where are Mom and Dad?" "They said they had a meeting in Ring One." I frowned. "Ring One? Why?" "They didn't explain." "When are they getting back?" "They said they didn't know." My brow rose in confusion. "*Okay.*" Something tugged at the edges of my thoughts. A meeting in Ring One? That wasn't normal. They ran their own company in Ring Three—most of their customers didn't look beyond Ring Two. Sure, there were a few from Ring One, but they'd never called for meetings. Not like this. And not on a Sunday. Sunday was sacred. Not just in faith, but in rhythm. In pause. Mom and Dad never broke it.

The television flicked on with a red screen in the other room—the color of danger, of warning. The familiar voice of Secretary O'Darle said robotically, "The Bureaucracy of the Third Dome City, Midas, has requested that you watch this mandatory viewing." Matthew and I drifted into the living room, dread pooling at our feet. What could the government want us to see?

The mandatory viewing screen disappeared, revealing the dismal gray Capitol building. A stone stage stood in front of it. President Xao Min stood front and center, his green eyes narrow and unblinking–like a snake sizing up its prey. Ever since I was little, I've found him unsettling. "Thank you for your participation, Midas. Though this city is the third of the twenty dome cities, *we* are the most prosperous. We have made ourselves number one. And I love our beautiful city. We have a wonderful system. But there are those who pose a threat to our society. Those who wish to see this city in ruins, who think the system is wrong. They would destroy our way of life as we know it! And I refuse to let that happen! But how do I know who wants to see us destroyed? Well, they have a fancy little name for themselves, those who belong to this radical ideology. A name that was supposed to have disappeared long ago with the war. Christians." The word struck me like a whip. I gasped, my heart stumbling into panic. What was happening? *Where were Mom and Dad?* President Min continued. "They hide among us, whispering words from an ancient, irrelevant book, claiming there is a better way to live, to serve their invisible god. They would have you doubt the Bureaucracy's leadership. They'll tell you that we intend to enslave everyone to our will. Their ideologies are the true slavery. Nothing but an old religion that was meant to be washed away by the blood of our ancestors, just like the rest of them. Our world doesn't need religion. Christians are obsolete. They were obsolete thousands of years ago. Yet they persist in going on. They continue to poison the minds of the people. Well! We won't let them taint the system any longer!" He pointed.

The camera's view widened. "No!" I cried out. Mom and Dad stood side by side on the stone stage. Guns aimed at their temples. "These are the leaders of a secret Christian organization! They've been hiding from us for twenty years, waiting for the chance to strike, like the snakes they are! And now, we will cut off the head!" He strode over to my parents. "Lucas," he addressed my dad. "You and Luciana have a very successful company. Rembrick Building Company is the highest building supply company in Midas. Many of the towers and shopping centres throughout this city are built with your company's products. Why betray the city you've lived in your entire life?" Dad remained unmoved. "I've not betrayed this city," Dad said. "Jesus Christ is the Way, the Truth, and the Life. I only ever wanted to give Midas life." President Min laughed. "We have a population of one million, and we always have. Midas is very much alive." "A city can be filled with people, but that does not mean it is alive." The president's face hardened. "Shut up!" He slapped him, then cleared his throat, regaining his composure. "Midas is a flourishing city. You are the one draining the life from it! The council wants to kill you, but *I* think you should have a chance." I sighed in relief. "Oh, please, God, let them live," I prayed. "If you reject your faith from this day on, you will be released." I held my breath. "I will never deny Jesus Christ, my Lord and Savior." He raised his voice to be heard from the back of the crowd. "*Jesus is King!*" He shouted, voice ringing over the crowd. Then the sound—final and merciless. His body collapsed like a string cut short. I screamed and clamped my hands over my ears, desperate to shut out the truth spilling across the screen. Dad was dead! I'd just watched him get shot! Matthew put an arm around me, holding me close. His face was pale; his eyes filled with terror.

President Min moved to Mom. "Luciana, the same goes for you. Think of your children out there. They're watching this. They just watched their father die. Will you make them orphans? Will you leave them to suffer alone?" Mom stared into his eyes with the coolness of a highly trained soldier. "They are not alone. God Almighty is a good Father, and He holds them still—in the palm of His hand." "Are you really willing to sacrifice them, too? Children need their mothers." "They will be cared for. They have each other. And they have people who will protect them. I am not afraid of you." "It's very easy, Luciana. Just renounce your faith, and I will let you go." Her eyes flared like fire. "You call us snakes, Xao Min. But even now, you are slithering, coiling up, prepared to strike. Hurl evil if you must—but the blood of those you've slain without cries louder than you ever could. You will not last, Xao Min. Before this year ends, your reign will rot." "*Silence!*" "You cannot silence El Shaddai! *The Lord God Almighty reigns!*" Her final cry echoed out through the screen, then she fell, and the world fractured again. I couldn't watch anymore. I rushed out of the room. My breath seized and broke into jagged pieces. Matthew followed close behind me and hugged me. I pushed against him in my panic. "Why?" I sobbed. "Why did they do it? We were safe. We were good. We were happy!" "I don't know, Elnora. I truly don't know." I tried to squirm from his hold. He grabbed my arms and held me still. "We have to get out of here," he said. I pushed away from him. "Why!?" "Because they're probably coming for us, too. We need to hide." I stepped back. My back touched the wall. My breathing was quick. "No. No. No. No, no, no, no, no, NO, NO! They can't do this to us, Matthew!! I don't wanna die!!" "Elnora, I know you're upset, but we have to get out of here. We need to find someplace safe." "Where?!" I cried. "There's nowhere! We can't leave Midas! No one can!" "Please, calm down. We need to think rationally if we're going to get out of here." I slid to the floor and began to cry. Matthew went upstairs, leaving me alone with my grief. "Why, God, why did you let this happen? We were happy. Why would you let them die?"

"Hello?" I shot up. Fear spiked through me. Someone was in the house! "Matthew! Elnora!" A feminine voice called to us. I ran upstairs. I had to hide! I couldn't die! Not today! "Please, don't be afraid! We're here to help you–your parents sent us!" I quietly closed the door to my room and hid in my closet. "Who are you?" Matthew called from his room. Did he want to die!? "We're from the church," the feminine voice answered. I heard some murmuring, but nothing clear for a few minutes. "Elnora! You can come out," Matthew called to me. I opened my door and came out. A woman with long, curly, artificial red hair stood at the bottom of the stairs. A younger woman stood beside her with short, light brown hair. Matthew was talking to them. "Hello, Elnora," the woman greeted me. "I'm Kat Perriwell. This is Dee Reed. We're from your parents' underground church, GIOR." "GIOR?" It sounded like a lifeline thrown into a storm. "It stands for God Is Our Refuge. Considering what happened to your parents, we're taking you there." "For how long?" Matthew asked. "Indefinitely." "Wait, what do you mean? We can't just disappear?" I questioned. Kat shook her head. "I'm afraid you have to. It's not safe for you to stay here. Please, grab anything you could need, so we can go." "How did you even get in here? I didn't hear the door." "Well, Elnora, your parents built a very secure access hatch to GIOR within the house. Your parents built it for emergencies." I turned to Matthew. "Do you think we should go with them?" "Yes, I think it would be best." I nodded, heart pounding. Matthew's voice carried our parents' strength, and I clung to it like a rope. "Okay, I'll go get my stuff."

I didn't know if their words were true. Matthew didn't either. But running meant believing–even if it was just believing in a chance. Maybe God had sent them. Maybe He was still watching over us, and I clung to that hope.

CHAPTER THREE

I packed my backpack with two changes of clothes, my Bible, and a hairbrush–just the essentials. I carefully removed our family photo from the hallway wall and tucked it inside. Unable to bear to leave it behind. I shouldered my pack and headed back downstairs. Matthew had finished packing already. "Ready to go?" Kat asked. I nodded. "Good. Come with me." She led us to, strangely, the coat closet, opened the door, and tapped a space in the left wall. To my surprise, a keypad fell. She put in a password, which triggered something under the floor. A handle popped up. She lifted it, revealing a secret passageway. "Has that been there the whole time?" Matthew asked. "Your parents had it installed when Elnora was a baby." "How did we not notice it?" "Well, it's not exactly easy to find, is it?" She climbed in. I looked at Matthew. How could we have missed this all along? When we were little, this was a typical hiding spot for hide and seek or a refuge to pout in. He offered me a sad smile but didn't say a word. He cast one look behind us before following Kat. I looked around one last time at the only home I'd ever known. My entire life. Would I truly never see it again? I stroked the doorway softly. Tears welled up, but I took a deep breath, readjusted my bag, and climbed in. The ladder was simply a long row of metal rungs. Dee followed after me but paused to relock the hatch.

"Hatch is secure, Miss Perriwell," she told her mentor with a thumbs up. I reached the bottom. The unmistakable stench of sewage filled my lungs. "Where are we?" I asked, covering my nose. "Beneath the city, in the sewer system. GIOR is further underground, but we have to go through the sewers to reach it. "Is it far?" Matthew asked. "Not very. There's a hatch about a mile from here."

Kat led us deeper in through a large canal and after nearly half an hour, she veered down a side tunnel. "Who's there?" a deep voice called out. A tall man with dark brown skin stepped into view, flashlight raised. "It's me, Hank. With Dee. And we've brought friends." He lowered his flashlight and looked at Matthew and me with wonder, like we were magical beings from a different dimension. "Can we come in?" Kat asked with an amused smile. He nodded. "Right, yes." He opened the hatch and stepped aside. "Thanks." Kat nudged him with her elbow. We climbed in. This ladder was shorter than the one that had led us into the sewers. Only a few feet. We stepped onto a dirt floor. I looked around. We were in a narrow hallway. The walls were also dirt. We followed Kat. Dee still kept up the rear. We stepped into the biggest room I've ever seen. It was enormous! It looked almost as big as the atrium of the Ring Two Shopping Centre. I froze in utter awe of the place. "Dee, will you get Jared?" Kat asked. She nodded and hurried off. "Pretty cool, huh?" I looked at Kat. "It's amazing! Did our parents build this?" "No, actually, this was a survival bunker during the Nuclear War. I don't know what they teach in schools these days, but every large city in the war had one of these. After the war, they built the dome cities over the old cities. Over Washington, D.C.'s remains, they constructed Cronus, the first dome city. They constructed Zeus, the second dome city, over New York City. They built our city, Midas, over Los Angeles." "Right, right. I just never really thought about the bunkers," Matthew said, still looking around in awe and wonder. "That's them!" I startled, heart jerking. Dee returned accompanied by a man, seemingly in his early thirties. He had dark brown hair, warm brown eyes, and stubble over his chin. "I'm Jared Brenwood," he introduced himself, shaking our hands. "You are Matthew and Elnora?" We nodded. He smiled. "I'm so glad to meet you both finally. My wife and I started coming after your parents decided to keep you both separated from GIOR." Matthew and I exchanged a sad smile. His face turned serious. "I'm so sorry all this has happened. You must be so confused." I nodded slowly. "We thought we were the only ones," Matthew told him. "Well, your mother was right when she said there would be people to protect you and take care of you. We're here for you. Now, if you'll follow me, I'll take you both to meet my family. My wife will be overjoyed to meet you." He turned to Kat and Dee. "Thanks for getting them here." "Thank you for giving us the pleasure of meeting them," Kat replied. Jared turned back to Matthew and me. "Come with me."

We followed him through the large common area that doubled as a cafeteria and lounge. He led us to some stairs that wound around to a large room, like an apartment. "Kate, I brought them!" A woman with short, golden-brown hair and warm dark eyes set aside a blanket she'd been sewing. She rushed over, an enormous smile on her face. "These are the heirs?" she asked excitedly. "Yes," he answered. "It's them." She hugged me. Her arms wrapping around me like a warm, comforting blanket after all that had just happened. "I'm so sorry, sweetie. It's awful what's happened. I understand if you might not feel like talking right now, but I'm here whenever you need me, okay?" I nodded, tears blinding my vision. "Thank you." She hugged Matthew and whispered something to him as well. She stepped back, still smiling. "I'm Kate—Kate Brenwood. You've met Jared, I'm his wife. These are two of our kids, Elliot and Emory." She pointed to the little boy and the baby playing on the floor. "I sent Elizabeth on an errand, but she should be back soon." "I'm right here." Kate yelped. "Lizzy! What have I told you about sneaking up on me?" The girl twisted her foot underneath her and kept her eyes on the floor; her long, black hair hung in her face. "Not to. Sorry, Momma." "It's alright, sweetie. These are Mr. Lucas and Miss Luci's kids, Matthew and Elnora. They are going to live here now." The girl glanced at both of us. Her ghostly blue eyes were so pale they looked nearly white. "Hi," I greeted her softly. She smiled at me nervously and waved her hand shyly. Kate turned to Jared. "Where will they be staying?" "The apartment beneath us," he told her. "Okay, great." She turned to us. "Did you bring anything with you?" "We took only what we could carry." She nodded. "Alright then. I'm sure we have plenty things in storage you both can use." She took a notepad from the counter and scribbled a list. "Elliot, will you run this to the Pattersons for me?" The boy jumped up and grabbed it. "Walking feet in the common area," she told him sternly. "Yes, Momma!" She turned back to us. "You must be full of questions." "Why does everyone keep calling us the heirs? And what exactly do you two do here?" Matthew asked. "Will we be here forever?" I asked, voice small. Jared and Kate exchanged glances. "Your parents were the leaders of GIOR. They ran this place together. They called you two "the heirs". You are the future leaders of GIOR," Jared explained. "Of course, this is your first time here. We're not putting you in charge now. Your parents had a plan for if/when they were discovered and killed called Project Co-heirs. You will join in many of the programs here in GIOR to help discover your gifts and grow you as the future leaders of the organization. They appointed Kate and me as leaders until you both mature and are ready to lead GIOR." Matthew and I just stood there wide eyed. This was crazy! "And the answer is no, Elnora. However, even though you and Matthew will be established as permanent residents down here, we will allow you to go to the surface when the time is right, but you will not return to your previous life." "So...what classes will we be taking? Will we be able to finish high school?" Matthew asked. "We're still figuring that out, but yes–you will finish high school. There are refugee teachers down here who can help finish your education. Your parents weren't clear about what classes you needed to take. And you both won't be taking all the same classes. It all depends on your natural giftings and what the Lord may want to use you for as leaders of GIOR." We both nodded in understanding. Jared added. "We'll be sending a team to your house tonight to look for anything your parents left behind for you two." Kate took a deep breath. "Now that we've sorted everything out. How about Jared shows you your apartment?" We started down the stairs. "Does everyone in GIOR live down here?" Matthew asked. "No, certainly not–but quite a few people do. Most GIOR members live above ground. We have about 1,500 members. Though I don't know how many will come tonight. They might be too afraid to come." "Do all the members have a secret hatch that leads here?" I asked. "Oh, no. That would completely devastate our limited funds. We only have four places– called Gospel Houses." "Wow, where are they?" "House Matthew is in Ring Six. House Mark is in Ring Four. House Luke is in Ring Three. And House John is in Ring Two. Some of those who come go to great lengths to get here." "I can see that. The last four rings are huge," I said. "Oh, yeah, I've been to Ring Six a couple of times. We actually lived in Ring Two before we moved down here." "Why did you?" I asked. "Kate was a hairdresser in Ring One. And I worked in the Capitol building. Kate got persecuted at work. One of her coworkers even filed a complaint with the government about her being a 'disruptor of the peace'. The authorities asked me to keep her contained, or they would 're-home' us in Ring Six. All she had been doing was sharing the Gospel with her coworkers and clients. We both agreed that she wouldn't stop. The message needed to be spread throughout the city, and we needed to do it. Then her coworker called the authorities and told them we were 'endangering' our children. Kate was pregnant with Emory. That's when we moved down here. We just needed to disappear." He opened a door at the bottom of the stairs. It was an identical apartment to the Brenwoods'. "Here we are! I know it's not much, but it should be quite comfortable." We walked in. It looked like something out of a sci-fi movie, but it looked nice. Besides, we were literally underground! "You two need anything else?" We shook our heads. "Alright." He smiled softly. "If either of you need anything, or just need to talk, Kate and I are here. We want to help you in any way we can. Just come on up. Okay?" We nodded. "Okay, dinner will be in a few hours. We'll come get you then." He closed the door, and we were alone.

Matthew looked at me. "How are you doing?" I shrugged. "I don't really feel anything right now. I feel empty and numb. I think I'm, honestly, still in shock." He nodded. "Me too." A moment passed. "So, what do you think of this place?" I looked around our apartment. "It's amazing, this place. I can't believe Mom and Dad hid this from us for years." "Yeah...it's pretty spectacular." "I like the Brenwoods," I said with a soft smile. "They seem nice." "Can you believe that all along there were other Christians? More people like us!" "It's great, I guess. But...why did Mom and Dad hide it from us?" I shrugged. "To protect us, I suppose. Maybe if we'd known, we would've been with them at the Capitol building. "Maybe, but it seems so strange for them. I mean, they fooled us into thinking we were the only ones our whole lives." "They never lied to us, though." "Did they?" Matthew started getting all puffed up. "They never told us the truth. They led us to believe a lie!" "Matthew, calm down! We'll figure this out." "It's not fair, Elnora! Why didn't they tell us the truth?" I put a hand on his arm. "We just have to believe that they meant well. They were our parents, after all. They were probably just trying to protect us." He sighed. And sank to the floor. "I want them to come back." Tears slid down his face. "I wish none of this had happened. Why did God let this happen?" I said nothing, at a loss for words. Of course, how should I know? God knew I felt the same as Matthew. Why would He let this happen? We needed our parents. A knock on the door. I ran over and opened it. Elliot stood there with two large tote bags full of stuff. "You look like you're going to topple over," I said as I took the bags from him. "Whoa, these are heavy. Did you really carry two of these?" He nodded proudly as I took the other. "Good work! Thank you! Now, you can go back home." He didn't leave, looking expectant. "D-did you want something?" He shook his head. "Do you need any help?" he asked. I smiled and shook my head. "No, but thank you." "Where's your brother?" "He's inside. He's okay. But-uh, why don't you go home now, so I can set up our beds." He nodded glumly. "Okay." He ran off. I brought the bags inside. Looks like Matthew had a little fan. He sat where he had been, staring off into space, his cheeks streaked with tears. His face showed utter devastation. "That was Elliot Brenwood." He didn't reply, instead hiding his face in his legs, quiet sobs occasionally coming out. I sighed and took blankets from the bags to begin making our beds.

A few hours later, as I sat trying to study my Bible to distract myself, another knock came to the door. Matthew was lying in bed, staring at the ceiling. I stood and went to the door. It was the Brenwoods. "It's almost time for dinner. Would you two like to join us?" Kate asked. I looked at Matthew. "Do you want dinner?" He shook his head. "I'm fine, thank you." I turned back to the Brenwoods. "Matthew isn't hungry, but I'll come." I wasn't hungry myself, but I desperately wanted to keep my mind busy. "Great!" They turned to walk to the common area. Kate whispered something to Jared. He nodded. Many tables filled the cafeteria. And they were mostly full. It was kind of comforting, knowing all of them believed the same as me. I sat next to Elizabeth at a table in the far corner. Jared set Emory down and went to the front. "Alright, everyone, you know the drill. Before we eat, we pray. Would you bow your heads?" We all did so. "Lord, we thank You for Your love for us. We thank You for protecting us from evil. We thank You for the time we had with Lucas and Luci. I ask for peace for the Rembrick kids. That You would be their comfort in this hard time. We thank You for this opportunity to eat and fellowship together. Please bless the food and the hands that prepared it. In Jesus' mighty name, Amen."

I lay on my bed, staring at the dark ceiling. Was Matthew asleep? I didn't know, but it had felt like hours since we'd gone to bed. My mind wouldn't go to sleep; over and over, it went through the events of today. I couldn't shut them off, no matter how hard I tried. Hours ago, I had run out of tears. I just lay there and spiraled down everything that had happened today. Why us? Why now? Why had God let this happen? I had so many questions, but it felt like none of them could be answered.

CHAPTER FOUR

"Elnora!" I turned around. I had just returned to the apartment after a shower. "Good morning, Jared," I greeted him cheerfully. "Good morning! I hope you slept alright? Did Kate show you the showers? Shaking my head, I replied. "I found it myself. I couldn't sleep, so I walked the halls a bit after I got sick of laying in bed." "I'm sorry to hear that. I have something I think is for you, though." He reached into his pocket and pulled out a piece of paper. "What is it?" "Looks like a note. The team found it taped to the door. Has Nora written on it?" I felt my stomach do a flip. The only person who had ever called me Nora–and I'd allowed it–was…. He handed it to me. "Thank you, Jared." My heart pounded. My chest tightened with nerves. "I hope it brings you a little hope in these dark times." I nodded and slipped back inside, the note clenched in my hand. Sitting down on my cot, I opened the note.

Nora,

I saw what happened on TV. Everyone did. It was awful. It's hard to believe someone as kind and lovely as you could be the daughter of two revolutionaries. I hope against hope that you didn't know what they were doing. I haven't been able to stop thinking about you since we left your house last night. If there's any chance that you'd be willing to speak to me tomorrow, I'd like to. I want to help you. I want to be your friend in this dark time. Please, Nora, let me in. I know we just met, but I feel like we're connected somehow. Like it's fate for us to know each other, perhaps more than that. I'm not sure if you could possibly feel the same way. But I'd like to hope you do. If you want to meet with me, come to the old manor on Copperman Street at four. I'll be waiting.

-Anthony

Anthony wanted to see me? He felt connected to me somehow? Could it be true? Surely, he was just messing with me. But...I *did* feel that way. Perhaps it was the Holy Spirit pushing us together to save Anthony! Yes! That had to be it. Something must be drawing him to my light. He wanted to understand it. And I could show him the truth!

I ran outside. "Jared!" He turned to face me. He was talking to a tall, muscular man I didn't recognize. "What's up?" "I need to get to Harminny House by four. Can I go?" He frowned. "Harminny House? Why?" "The note is from a friend–they saw what happened and feel awful. They want to meet me there. I can share the Gospel with them!" His face didn't change. "Can you tell me about this friend?" "They're from school," I told him. "They're very nice, and they're interested. They've seen the light in me! I've gotta go meet them, Jared! Please!" I was not one for pleading, but it seemed necessary. It was urgent, after all. He thought for a moment, then nodded. "We could get you there from the sewers. There is a direct line. But someone would have to go with you for protection. They would stay nearby, just in case you were in trouble." I squealed and hugged him. "Thanks, Jared!" He seemed bewildered but touched.

After breakfast, Jared led Matthew and me through the bunker. GIOR was enormous. I couldn't believe that this vast world had been hidden beneath the city I'd known all my life. It was amazing. First, he led us to a classroom. "This is where we teach the basics of salvation. It might feel simple at first, but Miss Carrington goes quite in depth. The class goes for four weeks. Five days a week at nine AM. We are constantly bringing people through here." "Oh, hi, Jared!" A woman with white-blonde hair in a braid and warm eyes placed her books down on the front desk. She walked over, eyes lighting up. "Are these them?" she asked. Jared nodded. "This is Matthew and Elnora." "It's so wonderful to meet you both." She hugged us. I smiled. She seemed genuinely happy; unlike most people you met in Midas. "Do you have anyone in your class right now?" She shook her head. "No, Destiny and Gavin graduated from the class last week. We'll start again tomorrow. I know it's a Tuesday, but we can just meet for a special class on Saturday, if that's okay?" Matthew and I nodded. "Great! See you both tomorrow then!" Next, we entered a gym-like room filled with activity–fighters sparring, guns going off. The man Jared talked with earlier directed the fighters. Across the room, a woman stood; it seemed to be a shooting range. Two people were shooting while she observed.

The people finished sparring, and the man noticed us as he turned around. "Jared!" "Hey, Michael," Jared waved. "How is everyone doing today?" "Great! We're training for the big mission on Saturday." He turned to Matthew and me. "And you two must be the heirs?" "That's us," Matthew said. I jumped when Matthew spoke. He'd been silent since last night. The man gestured, signaling the group behind him. They all lined up, except the female instructor, who stepped up beside him. "I'm Michael Castrow. This is my wife, Kendra. This is the Search and Rescue Team. Our son, Cal, Ezra Twickham, Diana Inkwell, Darcy Bennet, Miriam Longbourne, and Amy Merryweather. We call 'em Cal, Twick, Di, Doc, Mir, and Mox. Helps on missions." They all looked rather intimidating, especially Diana. She had short, straight black hair with two bright green stripes on the left side and serious, narrow gray eyes. She reminded me of the assassins I'd read about in the few fantasy books I'd read. "Say hi, everyone," Michael told them. "Hey!" They all said in unison. I offered a small wave, nerves buzzing. "We look forward to starting training for you two. We'll run assessments tomorrow at 10. That'll help us tailor your training." I nodded in understanding. Jared spoke up. "Now, if you'll excuse us, Michael. I gotta show them the other classes." "Of course! See you guys later!"

By the end of the tour, we found we had four classes. After Gospel 101 and Search and Rescue training, we had the History of Christianity, and the last class would be our normal education. Though after we finished Gospel 101, there would be more advanced classes to take. Now I sat in the apartment, thinking. This place was unlike anything I knew. Though, of course, I'd never left Midas, so anything outside of that was new. I skipped lunch, despite Jared persuading Matthew to eat. He'd been so quiet all day. I mean, we were both grieving. Naturally, neither of us was being our normal selves, but...we were best friends. Surely, it would be easier to fight this sadness together. That's when I thought of Jenn. The execution viewing had been mandatory. She must've seen it. What had she thought of it? She had met my parents. We'd had the Dillons over so many times. Jenn surely couldn't believe that my parents had been rebels trying to take over the city. Could she? Oh, how I wished I could talk to her right now! Matthew came in. "Hey," I greeted him softly. "Hey." "How was it?" He shrugged. "It was good, I guess. Didn't really notice." "Oh." "Did you talk with Jared?" "A little. He seems like a nice guy." I smiled softly. "Yeah, he does." "He said you were meeting someone later. Who?" "Oh, just someone from school." "Jenn?" I shook my head. "No, a-uh new friend." "Oh. Okay." His brow furrowed–but he asked nothing. He just nodded and looked away. I couldn't tell him I was going to meet a boy–especially Anthony–whom we both scarcely knew. He would never let me go. Say it was dangerous. But Anthony wouldn't hurt me. He was a gentleman.

I met Jared at the hatch that went into the sewers above us. Diana was with him. Jared waved. "Hey, you remember Diana from earlier? She'll be escorting you to Harminny House." "Okay." "Ready to go?" she asked. I nodded. "Good. Let's go." She keyed in a password. The hatch beeped, unlocked, and we climbed up the ladder. "Hey, Di," a man with well-kempt gray hair and weathered brown eyes greeted her. "Hey, Stephen." She helped me up. "Where you goin'?" "Taking one of the heirs to meet someone. Stay safe, will ya?" She lightly punched him in the shoulder. "Back at ya," he replied. She turned to me. "Come on." I followed her through the sewers. The sewers stretched like an endless maze–rank, wet, and winding. It felt like ages before we turned down a small alleyway to a hatch. "This hatch will open in the Harminny House basement," Diana told me. "Take this." She handed me a small device. "Click the button on that if you're in trouble. I'll come running." I nodded. "Thank you." I climbed up the ladder, carefully lifted the lid, slid it aside, and climbed out. I looked around. This was definitely a basement–dusty, dark, and forgotten. I walked up the ancient wooden stairs and opened the door to the main level of the dilapidated mansion. Harminny House used to be the mayor's manor. Mayors governed each ring until about a hundred years ago, when President Lyndon Tzar disbanded them, placing all rings under the main executive government. All the manors fell into ruin and disrepair, left abandoned. I heard a door open. "Anthony," I called. I ran towards the noise, and there he was. "Nora!" To my shock, he ran up and pulled me into a bear hug. "I'm so glad to see you're alive." "Me too." "Where were you? I was so scared when no one answered the door yesterday. How did you get my

44

letter?" I stared at the carpet, brushing it nervously with my foot. "For safety reasons, I can't tell you. But some friends got the letter for me. Thank you, Anthony." He smiled. "Come on, sit down." He gestured to a pair of old antique dining chairs. "What did you want to talk about?" I asked nervously. He took a deep breath. "Look, I know you felt it. From the moment we met, we had a connection." I froze. "You're the only girl who has noticeably been attracted to me but hasn't fawned over me. Most girls make themselves ridiculous to get a guy's attention, but not you; you were just yourself, no matter what. Do you know how attractive that is?" I felt myself blush, keeping my gaze fixed on a slit in the floor. He got up and came closer. He kneeled and put a hand to my cheek. "I want you, Nora. More than you know." My heart beat rapidly. "I can't, Anthony," I said. His eyes darkened. "Why not?" I shook my head. "W-we don't have the same ideas of how a relationship should be handled before marriage." "I'll do whatever you want me to, Nora." His eyes were lit with passion. "I'm totally captivated by you." Oh, if I could've melted into a puddle, I would've. "Will you really do whatever I want?" I asked with a shy smile. He nodded. "I swear it." I laughed and nodded. "Okay." He smiled, looking like he'd won the world, and stood up. "Okay, so what do you want to do?" "Well, you see, my family has always had some guidelines." "Family? But your parents are dead." That stung–but not enough to make me turn back. "I'd still like to follow them. It's what I was raised with. I'd prefer to stick with it." He sighed. "Okay." My gut said there was already too much wrong with this, but my heart couldn't walk away. "First, um...," I chuckled nervously. "I won't do-um...you know." He smirked. "Yeah, I know what you're talking about." I smiled. "Thanks." "What else?" I thought for a moment and couldn't think of anything else. "Well, just...if I say I'm uncomfortable with something, I want you to listen, even if it's silly." He nodded. "I'm not a terrible person, Nora. No matter what your brother has led you to believe about me." I blinked. "What are you talking about? Matthew hasn't said anything bad about you." He shrugged. "He noticed our connection and told me to back off. That you were too innocent for me. I'm glad you've come to your own conclusions, though." I smirked. "Matthew's just overprotective. He still treats me like I'm ten." I wanted to smack myself. What did I just say? That's not what Matthew thought at all! What possessed me to say that? Anthony chuckled. "Thought so. Good job breaking away from his control." Guilt clawed at my stomach. He checked his watch, then brushed the back of his head. "Well, I gotta get going. My parents will be expecting me home from school." I smiled. "Okay." He hugged me tightly. "When can I see you again?" "How about the same time next week?" "I'll clear my schedule." I laughed. He released me. "See you later. Stay safe." "Thanks. You too, Anthony." He left. I returned to the basement and descended into the sewers. "Welcome back! I was about to come up anyway. You sure took your sweet time." I felt myself blushing. "Sorry, Diana." "What's going on?" she asked suspiciously. "Oh, just a friend wanted to see me. They saw my parents' execution and wanted to hear about the Gospel." What was happening?! Why was I lying!?

46

She didn't seem too sure about it but didn't question further as we returned to GIOR.

"How'd it go?" Matthew asked as I walked into the apartment. "Good!" I answered, praying he couldn't tell I'd just come from seeing Anthony. If what he'd said was true, Matthew wouldn't be pleased to hear that I had just been with him–alone. "Were they receptive to what you had to say?" "Yeah, definitely. I think we made good progress." I added a smile for good measure. "We're meeting again next week." "That's great! I'm proud of you, Elnora." "Thanks," I muttered, gut sinking under the weight of guilt. It was fine. As soon as Anthony came to Christ, Matthew wouldn't care that I'd been seeing him behind his back. Everything would be just fine! There was no reason to worry!

CHAPTER FIVE

"John 1:1-5 is one of the clearest expressions of the Gospel," Miss Carrington began. "It starts with explaining exactly who Jesus is. All four of the Gospels do this in their own way. Matthew shows His genealogy, Mark highlights His uniqueness, especially through His baptism, and Luke explores His birth and glimpses of His childhood, but John contrasts so differently from the other three Gospels. Let's take a look at what he writes, shall we?" I flipped to it in my Bible. "*In the beginning was the Word, and the Word was with God, and the Word was God. He was in the beginning with God. All things came into being through Him, and apart from Him, not even one thing came into being that has come into being. In Him was life, and the life was the Light of mankind. And the Light shines in the darkness, and the darkness did not grasp it.*" Miss Carrington gently set down her Bible, her expression glowing with warmth. "Isn't that beautiful? What do you notice about that? What can you tell me about Jesus from those five verses?" I raised my hand. "Jesus was life and light, and He brought it to the world." Miss Carrington smiled. "Very good, Elnora. Jesus was life. Let's note that." She wrote that on the chalkboard. "Now let's change that to Jesus *is* life. Because even though Jesus ascended to Heaven thousands of years ago, His sacrifice continues to bring life to people every day." She paused and smiled with shining eyes. "Isn't that beautiful? Many places in the Bible does it say that Jesus is life. Not that He was, or used to be, but that He is. Now, I want to show you what I think is the Gospel summarized in a single verse. Let's turn to John 3:16." I and the other students did so. *"For God so loved the world, that He gave His only Son, so that everyone who believes in Him will not perish, but have eternal life."* She beamed at the class. "There it is–plain and powerful. That's exactly what the Gospel is. God sent Jesus to this world because He loved us, and when we have faith in that, we will have eternal life. Isn't that wonderful?" I smiled. Miss Carrington had a unique quality from other teachers. She wasn't just reciting lessons from a guidebook. No, it was much deeper than that. She was passionate about what she taught. She loved what she taught. And who could blame her?

"What did you think of that?" I asked Matthew as we walked towards the training center. "Fine, I guess." "She was so passionate," I added, still amazed. "I don't think talking about the Bible should make someone that excited. It needs to be taken more seriously. I'm going to talk to Jared about it." I blinked. What? Was it wrong to be passionate about the Bible? What was wrong with joy? I responded, "Oh," speechless. We walked into the training center. It was empty. "Where is everyone?" Matthew asked Michael as he walked over. "Oh, we rarely train on Tuesdays. Most of them don't live down here, and we all have jobs. We don't even live down here. We live in Ring Three." "What? You guys live in Ring Three?" I exclaimed. "How come we've never seen you before?" "Ring Three is pretty big, isn't it?" I shook my head. It was so strange. The Castrows lived in Ring Three, but we never met. Mom and Dad had never invited them over—why? If they had similar beliefs, wouldn't they have wanted their kids close to them? "Cal goes to Ring Three High," Kendra said. "I was surprised that neither of you had crossed paths with him." "Wait–he's *that* Cal Castrow?" Matthew gaped. I jumped in. "The one that all the girls are crazy about?" They laughed. "He's always said the girls have always been acted pretty silly around him," Michael said. "Drives him nuts," Kendra added, twirling a finger at her temple. "Alright, well, enough talk. I have to prepare the simulator. We'll start with you, okay, Matthew?" she said. He nodded. "Yes, ma'am." We approached a massive metal chamber. "Since a lot of our team works and even Cal has school, this simulator has been really great for training. And it's especially nice for evaluating. We can see everything via this screen, and you can't actually get hurt." Kendra tapped some things into the keypad. She fired off questions–random ones, or so they seemed. "Alright, the first evaluation will be physical, the next will be mental. This computer here will show me exactly what you're seeing." She pushed a button, and a metal door opened. "Go on," she told him. He walked in. The door closed. "Ready?" she asked him. He nodded and gave her a thumbs up. "Physical evaluation beginning in 3, 2, 1." I watched as a jungle spread throughout the box in a lifelike way. A large black cat jumped out of the bushes and tackled him. He wrestled the cat, using all his strength to throw it off. I lunged toward the screen, instinct screaming to pull him out. "It's okay, Elnora," Michael said. I looked at him. He put an arm around me. "It can be scary," he said gently. "But he's completely safe." "Thanks," I whispered. After a couple of minutes, Matthew had finally taken down the big cat, his breath ragged. Kendra announced in the small microphone, "Mental evaluation beginning in 3, 2, 1." "This can be really hard to watch," Michael explained. "Why?" Matthew's expression twisted into pure terror. He backed himself against the wall and extended his arms out. He screamed. I covered my ears, heart racing. "What is it doing to him?" I asked. And then I saw millions of tiny insects crawling on the walls and floor and onto Matthew. I nearly laughed–of course it would be bugs. He always hated them.

When Matthew came out, he was panting. He turned to Kendra. "That was crazy! Were you trying to kill me?" He gasped. She shook her head. "I was evaluating your physical and mental strength. What did you think it was going to be like?" "I don't know! Just not nearly giving me a heart attack and not getting beat up. It might've been a simulation, but it certainly felt real. Come on, Elnora!" I just stared after him, too stunned to follow. He looked back. "Come on!" I stared at the ground and crossed my arms. "Can't I just try?" He shook his head. "If I couldn't handle it, you won't either!" I still didn't move. "I don't know what's wrong with you, Matthew. But I don't care if you think I can't handle it. I'm going to do it." I turned to Kendra. "Put me in." She smirked. "You're tougher than I thought."

She turned to the keyboard. Matthew groaned. "You're letting her go through with this?" "You're her brother, not her parent, and all things considered, your parents put the two of you in the Brenwoods's care, and Jared requested that you both do this." He threw his hands in the air. "Fine! But don't come to me crying if you're paralyzed from what you go through." Michael chuckled. "What's so funny?" he asked. "They all act this way at first. We've just never done siblings before. They always bounce back after a couple of days." Matthew's face turned blank. "That's insane! Do you seriously enjoy torturing people who just want to help GIOR?" "It doesn't hurt anyone. It never has. It's just a test and a simulation," Kendra explained, turning back to the tablet. She asked me the same questions. "Have you had any physical training of any kind?" "No." "Not even sports?" "No, never interested me." "What do you remember most about your last dream?" "I-uh-I was at my old house, only it was all in gray tones." "What would you say your greatest strength is?" "I, er, I think I'm very nice. T-to everyone." "Greatest weakness?" I think long and hard. "I don't know." She smiled at me. "Alright, go on in. Good luck!" "Thanks." The door opened, and I walked in.

Suddenly, the black room illuminated, and I found myself standing by the Capitol building, surrounded by a shouting crowd. I maneuvered through the crowd to investigate, but then someone seized me and tackled me to the ground. A man I didn't recognize—his face twisted with rage. I tried to roll him off, but he was too heavy—solid as stone. His hands went to my throat. I grabbed them and pushed him back. My unexpected brute strength startled him, and I rolled away and jumped up. My heart thundered. Adrenaline lit up every nerve. He reached for me again, but I bounced to the side and climbed onto his back and wrapped my arm around his neck, pulling tight. He fell to the ground, knocking the wind out of me. Then everything faded away.

Now I was in a dark room. The room began to close in on me. Panic surged like a wave. My breath quickened. Where was the door!? I felt along the walls frantically. No door. My chest slammed with each terrified heartbeat. I tripped. A crowbar sat in the room's center. I grabbed it with shaky hands and hooked it under the rapidly closing wall. I pushed once. Again. A third time. And just as the walls squeezed against my shoulders, "Simulation complete." Now I was sitting in the middle of the black room. The door opened, and I rushed out. Michael laughed. Kendra smirked. Matthew stood pale, jaw slack. "What? What'd I do?" "You completely threw us off with your reactions," Kendra explained. "We were not expecting you to react the way you did. With such action. You were phenomenal." I blushed, murmuring, "Thanks." "You were great," Michael exclaimed. "What was so crazy about what I did?" "For the physical, you were resilient and used your slight frame to your advantage." I shrugged. "I wasn't even really thinking. I was just going off of reaction." Kendra looked at me with a quizzical expression. "What about the mental? I had your heart rate. I could see what you were feeling. But you only sat there for a second." "I guess it was the same for that–I just reacted to whatever was happening." Michael rubbed my shoulder. "We'll be proud to have you join us for training tomorrow." He looked at Matthew. "Both of you. Great job today." The bell rang for lunch. "Well, see you guys later," Michael said. "Kendra and I gotta get to work."

I lay in bed, staring up at the ceiling. The same thing all over again. The weight of it all returned, heavy and quiet. Tears slowly fell down my face. I wanted Mom. Everything in me wished for her to come sit on my bed and hug me. I wanted her to tell me it would be alright. That everything would be okay. That this was only a nightmare. But it wasn't, and I would never see her again. I missed home. But we could never go back. And it's not like it would ever really feel like home again. Even though I'd lived there my entire life, it would never feel like home without Mom and Dad.

"Alright, everyone," Michael called to everyone in the training center as we walked in. After the evaluations, Kendra had handed us both matching black jumpsuits, white stripes running down the sides. Everyone else wore the same–including Michael, who was so muscular I couldn't believe there was one that could fit him. Everyone lined up in front of him. "You've met Matthew and Elnora Rembrick. They will join us from now on. And of course, we have nicknames for them!" The group cheered and whooped. He moved over to Matthew and put his hand on his shoulder. "This is The Brother, but we will call him Bro." He laughed. "He's loyal and protective of those he cares about." Matthew shot him a glare–he still thought the Castrows' methods were too extreme. I hadn't seen everything he'd gone through in the simulator, but something had terrified him. Michael moved over to me. "And this is Pipsqueak. She may be small and gentle, but she's tough when it counts. Please welcome, Pip!" They cheered. Kendra glanced at Michael, nodded, and turned to the others. Michael urged us to stand with them. I ended up between Matthew and the blonde girl–what was her name again? It escaped me. "Alright, we have a mission coming up. As you know, the authorities took Dr. Nikea Freeman on Monday. For those of you who don't know, she was a scientist in the Ring One Science Experimentation Division, but she was also spying for GIOR. The authorities plan to execute her on Saturday. We will go in on Friday night. So, we have today and tomorrow to prepare. Any questions?" I raised my hand. "Will Matthew and I be doing it too?" "That entirely depends on your progress. All that's really important is that you know how to shoot *well* and can take orders. This is a fairly easy mission. Doc, you will lead it. You can choose a second in command, or we can assign one." Doc nodded. "I'll take care of it," he replied. "Great! Let us know before the mission, though. Right, Ezra?" The dark-haired young man brushed the back of his head. "Okay, okay, it was my first time leading the mission." "And because you failed to communicate, you haven't led another mission in three months." "Hey, at least you've led a mission. Amy

55

has never been the leader." The blonde girl cried out. "I would if you would just make me the leader! You two are in charge!" "Well, we need someone to fly the transport. You're the only one who knows how to fly." She rolled her eyes. "You're a pilot?" I asked her. She grinned. "Yep!" "You've left Midas?" She nodded. "Yep, most of my flights are between here and Cronus, Zeus, or Oedipus. Mostly Oedipus." "What are they like?" "Bigger, but the same." "Is it dangerous to fly?" "As much as it was before the war, I'd guess." "But–but what about the chemicals? From the war, I mean." She shook her head. "I don't know what those schools teach, but it's not dangerous out there." "But what about the clouds? They're orange, aren't they?" She laughed. "No! They're the same color as the clouds that they project on the dome. The government is just scaring all the kids to keep them in line. They told you the ground outside was poison, too, I'll bet. That's what they told me." "Is it?" She shrugged. "Don't know. I'm only allowed to fly over it. I'd guess the ground isn't poisoned if the sky isn't." "Have you seen the ocean?" She nodded. "That's the one thing they weren't lying about. It's sad, isn't it? We're not allowed to fly over it. The fumes would kill anyone. It's awful. Midas is right next to the ocean, but no one can see it. No one would know it's even there if they hadn't shown us a map." "Alright, everyone! Quit chatting! We have some training to do! Miriam, Ezra, take Elnora over to the shooting range. Doc, Diana, you two spar. Amy, you will spar with Kendra. Cal, you'll help me work on Matthew." A woman with light brown curly hair in a ponytail and soft gray eyes, and the dark-haired young man came over to me. "Heya, Pip!" He held out his hand to me. "Hi, you're Ezra, right?" I shook his hand. "Yup, Ezra Twickham." "It is wonderful that you and your brother have joined the team, Elnora," the woman said. "Thank you." We walked over to the shooting range. Ezra picked up a gun. "They're not real, but they pack a punch." I took it. Woah! It was heavy! I lifted it. "You need to work out, Pip," he said. "Get some meat on those arms." Miriam helped me put the gun in position. "You got it?" I nodded. She lifted her own gun. "Just watch me." She pressed a button on the side and pulled the trigger. A big bang rang out. "They're not real bullets. Just BB's," Twick explained. I pressed the red button, and green energy pulsed through it. I pulled the trigger. The gun quickly pushed back. "Good job! You nearly hit the bullseye," Miriam exclaimed. I let the gun down. The white ring just outside the bullseye showed the bullet hole. Wow! "You're a natural, Pip!" I smiled. "Thanks." "Alright, let's do it a few more times, so you can get the hang of it."

"Great work, everyone! We've made some great progress over the past couple of days," Michael said. "Kendra and I are very proud of you all, especially our new recruits." Matthew and I stood in line with the rest of the team. I smiled. "Now, whether you can join the mission. It was a carefully made decision. And Elnora and Matthew will be going." I beamed. I was going on a mission! "Everyone meet here at 12:30 tomorrow afternoon, and we'll prepare to head out. Dismissed!" Cheers erupted around me. "Great job, Elnora," Amy cheered as she hugged me. The others gathered to offer encouragement–smiles, high fives, and proud nods. Matthew and I stood in the center, swept up in a wave of affirmation. I couldn't believe it. I was actually going on a mission.

CHAPTER SIX

Friday morning, Matthew and I completed our classes. We were about to head to the training center for some extra shooting practice before the mission when Jared ran up to us. "Are you two busy?" I shook my head. "What is it?" "The Castrows just returned from doing some more thorough investigation of your house. They discovered some things you should see." We glanced at each other in curiosity, then followed Jared to the Brenwoods' apartment. Kate was sitting with Elliot and Elizabeth at the table while Emory played on the floor next to them. She looked up. She spoke to Elizabeth. "Take Elliot and Emory into the other room, please?" The girl nodded and whispered something to Elliot before scooping up Emory and rushing into the other room. "Please sit down." Matthew and I sat at the table. "Jared said the Castrows found something at our house." Kate nodded. "Yes." She picked up a folded piece of paper. "Alright, so, as Jared explained, Michael and Kendra did some extensive digging at your house, and they found some very eye-opening stuff." She put a small box on the table. She opened it. "This is what they found." She pulled out two envelopes. "These are for you two. It has your names on them." She handed them to us. Seeing our names written in Mom's handwriting, tears threatened to spill. I urged them away. It was so silly.

It was just her handwriting. "They also found this." She pulled out a slip of paper. "It's a restraining order for a Miss Elspeth Briar Rembrick." Aunt Elspeth! "That's our aunt. She's not like us; she left the faith and didn't just become a normal person like the rest of Midas," I started. "She's an alcoholic," Matthew explained. "We haven't seen her in years. And the law states that in the case of the death of both parents, the closest living relative will become the child's legal guardian. Our parents wouldn't trust Aunt Elspeth with a dog." Kate and Jared nodded. "That's actually the next thing we need to show you both. There was a letter on the ground in front of the front door from your aunt. She wants to see you at least, if not come live with her. However, seeing as there is documentation against it, we definitely will not be allowing that. Do you two have many memories of her, or was she removed from your life earlier in your lives?" I shrugged, not wanting to remember what I could of her.

It was strange that she and Dad had been raised in the same family with the same beliefs. When Matthew and I were little, Aunt Elspeth came over often. But it never ended well. When the screaming and cussing started, Mom had rushed us upstairs, but it was hard not to hear. Aunt Elspeth had called Dad and Grandpa awful things. She told Mom often that she needed to run while she still could. Whatever that meant. She said if God were real, He was cruel, enjoying seeing people suffer. Like a kid burning ants with a magnifying glass. Dad always said Aunt Elspeth had something unthinkably horrible happen to her when she was a teenager. That when she had been a child, she had been the sweetest girl. Dad had often said that I was a lot like her. But after that horrible thing happened, she hadn't been able to continue being that innocent girl. And it was very sad, and we needed to pray for her every day. Then one night, I remembered she had broken into the house, grabbed me out of my bed, and taken me to her house. She claimed I would be better off with her. That she could give me the life I deserved. But I couldn't stop crying. That was the day Aunt Elspeth went to jail. It was so sad.

I finally spoke up. "She kidnapped me when I was five. She was arrested the very next day. That's when our parents got the restraining order on her, I would guess, or maybe upon her release. Because we haven't seen her since then." The Brenwoods looked at each other, then back at us. "I'm sorry that happened." I shrugged. "I hardly remember it." "Well, thank you for explaining some things. I know you're both on the rescue mission tonight. Aim well, stay safe." I thanked him. Before we left, Kate hugged me. "If you ever need anything, I'm here. Don't hesitate to come here whenever you need a friend." "I will, Kate. Thank you." I sat on my cot and looked at the two letters. I opened Mom's and read it:

My dear Elnora,

I'm sure that whatever has happened has left you very
confused. I'm sorry I'm not there to comfort you in
person. But things will never be the same. There are
things that Dad and I hid from you and Matthew for
your safety. If you don't know about it now, then you
will soon. You can trust these people, and GIOR
needs you and Matthew. You both are exceedingly
gifted. And you two are blessed because you are the
only people in the entire organization to have been
raised in the Word of God. But before anything else,
you need to know this: you were chosen. Chosen from
the very beginning by God to do something amazing.
Never doubt who you are in Him. He wants to use
you; just be open to His calling. You have always been
very special. You want everyone to come to believe,
but you do not shout or threaten hell on everyone.
You do not even have to tell them you are a Christian;
they can just tell by how you live. By your grace, your
gentleness, and your kindness. Someday, I think Jenn
will see the truth. I know it may seem hopeless since
you have been friends for so long, but you just have to
keep shining. But there is more you need to know.
Never compromise your morals to bring the light to
someone. It is dangerous and could get you seriously
hurt. I know it's hard when no one else seems to have
the same beliefs and you so desperately want to save
them. But it's a slippery slope. Oh, my sweet Elnora! I
wish I were with you right now! Do not give up! God
has chosen your generation. We have always known it.

To bring the dome cities to Him. I wish we could see it. But if you are reading this, then it was God's plan that you and Matthew are on your own. Never doubt yourself. Hold your brother up. He needs you more than he will admit. Don't let him push you away. You are so strong together. Did we ever tell you what your name meant? It was with significance that we named you Elnora Elizabeth. Elnora means compassion. Elizabeth means pledged to God. It could not be more perfect for you. You are the most compassionate person I've ever met. And you have always been so dedicated to your faith. Never lose that compassion. Never lose that dedication. They will serve you. Believe me. I love you. You are the greatest daughter I could've ever been gifted with. I thank God for you every day. Never lose hope. Never give up.

Love,

Mom

Tears were falling down my face. Oh Mom! I wish you were here! I buried my face in my pillow and let the sobs come. I wanted to scream. How could they kill her!? How could they kill Dad!? They did nothing! They just loved us! They loved anyone who would let them. Even some that wouldn't let them. Like Aunt Elspeth. They tried to show people God even in their deaths. Lord, why!? Why did You let this happen!? We needed them! And now they're gone! Why did You take them from us!? I felt Matthew stroke my shoulder. I sat up and hugged him, still sobbing. "Why, Matthew?" "I don't know. But we have to trust God knows what He's doing. Because He does." "But why did He have to take them from us?" "Your guess is as good as mine." His voice wavered. "But we have each other. We have GIOR. Things could be a lot worse." "I know. I just really miss them." "Me too." I couldn't find any more words. I just cried while Matthew held me and shed tears of his own. We would fight this grief together, even when it's hard.

A knock on the door woke me up. I sat up in bed and wiped the tears from my eyes. Matthew had gone to do some target practice. I stood up and groggily went over to the door. I opened it. Amy stood there. She smiled sadly. "Hey, Elnora." "Hey." "You look terrible." I wiped another hand over my face. "I read a letter my mom wrote before..." "You want a hug?" I nodded. She wrapped her arms around me. I clung to her. I had desperately wanted a sister when I was younger. Was this what it was like? She released me and cleared her throat. "The Castrows sent me. It's time to get ready." I nodded. "I'm coming." She smiled. "Great, get changed. I'll wait here."

We entered the training center. Ezra came over. "Hey, Pip! Ready to go?" I nodded. "Let's go, Twick!" "Yeah! That's what I like to hear!" He high fived me. "Good to see you, Elnora," Michael said. I got in line between Ezra and Amy. "Alright, everyone," Kendra stood in front of a large computer screen. "Dr. Freeman is in detention level three of the detainment facility. We don't know which cell. I'll be here hacking the cameras. Remember, avoid as much loss of life as you can without risking your own lives. Any questions?" Silence. "Great! Michael, would you pray?" He nodded. "Let's circle up, everyone." We gathered around the Castrows. "Lord, we thank you for your love and grace. We thank you for this opportunity to rescue Dr. Freeman. We ask that you would protect us in this time of great danger. Your Word says, 'we will not need to fear the terror of the night or the deadly pestilence' because you will protect us, and so we ask you to do this now. Please, bring everyone back safely. In Jesus' name. Amen.

Amy jumped into the transport and started it up. She checked everything, then gave us a thumbs up. We all jumped in. "Hold on, Pip," Ezra said. The helicopter rose. I wobbled and for a moment I thought I was going to fall. "Careful!" Someone grabbed me and held me close. But it wasn't Ezra when I looked up. It was Cal. The Castrows' son was the spitting image of Michael; except he had dark blond hair. I looked up at him. He was very tall. "Thanks." "No problem." He smiled softly. His blue eyes held an unreadable expression that gave me a warm, fuzzy feeling.

Amy's voice came over a speaker, loud and clear. "Alright, everyone, we're heading out!" The helicopter rose higher and higher. We came out of a hatch. Cool air hit my face. It was the first time I'd been above ground since Monday, the first time I'd been outside since Saturday. Cal still held me tight, his muscular arms holding me close against him. Now we were above the city. It was beautiful. Lights flickering from the skyscrapers in Ring One and Two, and the small amount in Ring Three.

"We're almost to the detention facility. Get ready to jump, people," Amy said over the intercom. "You ready, Pip?" Cal asked me. "Ready as I'll ever be," I replied. Dr. Bennet came over to the edge, looked beneath the transport, then called. "Line up!" We did so. We came closer to the building. Fear spread through me. WE WERE JUMPING FROM A HELICOPTER!? No one had told me we were doing this! "This is crazy!" Matthew exclaimed. "It's okay. Don't worry about landing. I'll catch you," Cal told me. "How? We're jumping at the same time!" "Just trust me, okay?" I nodded. "Jumping in 3, 2, 1!" Dr. Bennet jumped, followed by Diana, Miriam, Ezra, Cal, and finally me. Sure enough, just before I fell, Cal caught me and rolled. "You okay?" he asked. I laughed. "Yep! Thanks!" I sat up. "No problem!" "Good job, everyone," Dr. Bennet said. "Guns at the ready!" I adjusted my gun in the way Miriam had taught me. "Di, get the lock." Diana ran over to the emergency exit. She pulled out a circular mechanism. She stuck it to the door over the keypad. It beeped. She pushed a button. It beeped again. She took it off and opened the door with ease. "After you, Doc," she told him with a smirk. He ran through. "Alright, we're clear. Let's move," he called after us. We rushed in, our boots clattering on the floor. We ran down the stairs. When we reached the door to Detention Level Three, Dr. Bennet opened it and scanned the hallway. "Clear!" We ran out the door. The hallway was white and pristine. This was a prison? "Intruders, stay your weapons!" I whipped around, gun at the ready. Two men came running after us. We've been spotted, Doc," Miriam called. I pulled the trigger. A tranquilizer dart shot into his leg. We didn't use real bullets if possible. Just tranquilizer darts that numbed people. Ezra shot right after me. Both men fell to the ground, completely numb. "I'll stay here to guard," Ezra said. He waved his hand. "Cal, help me guard this entrance!" Cal ran over. I ran down the hallway after the others. I heard more gunshots from behind and ahead of me. Panic coursed through me, but I had to keep going. "Dr. Freeman!" Dr. Bennet moved over to a cell. "Darcy!" "Get the door, Di." Diana took a small pistol from a holster on her side and shot the bottom lock and top lock. She twirled it and put it back in her holster. Apparently, it had real bullets in it. Doc slid the door open. "Are you hurt?" he asked the woman. She had short, straight, black hair, dark brown skin, and brown eyes. She shook her head. "They roughed me up a little bit, but it's nothing compared to what they've done to others." She had a similar accent to Dr. Bennet. I wondered where they were from to get such different accents. They couldn't possibly be from Midas. "Alright, let's get out of here," Dr. Bennet said. We ran down the hall. Diana and Miriam covered us from behind. Dr. Bennet, Dr. Freeman, and I hurried down the hall. Ezra and Cal stood by the door, guns held up to shoot. "Heading out," Dr. Bennet told them.

"Got it," Ezra said. Dr. Bennet put Dr. Freeman on his back. I followed, then Miriam, Diana, Matthew, Cal, and Ezra. We ran up the stairs at what seemed like an impossible speed. I was surprised I could even keep up, but the panic and adrenaline shooting through me made it easy. We reached the top. Dr. Bennet pressed a button on his earpiece. I didn't even know he had one. "Touch down, Mox!" "On my way," her voice came back. The silent transport flew over next to the building. Dr. Bennet readjusted Dr. Freeman from his back to his arms, then jumped into the helicopter. Miriam followed, then Ezra, Diana, and Matthew. I came to the edge. "You got this, Pip," Cal said. I jumped and landed hard on the floor of the transport. He followed. My shoulder throbbed from the impact. "Well done, everyone," Dr. Bennet said. "Mission accomplished." Diana put a hand on my shoulder. "You did good, newbie." I smiled. "Thanks." She moved over to Dr. Bennet. I did it! I really did it! As a part of the Search and Rescue team, I saved someone. I had shot a gun. I hadn't hesitated. I was so thrilled. If only I could tell Anthony, he would've been so excited. But he couldn't know. Not until he changed.

CHAPTER SEVEN

Things fell into line after that. Each day mirrored the last, with classes and training, and I started meeting with Kate every afternoon. She was so kind and a great listener, and I felt like I was learning a lot from her, too. And on Tuesdays, I met with Anthony for an hour at Harminny House. Every evening there were devotionals led by different high-standing members. They were really interesting and impactful. And things were going just so well with Anthony. Every time we saw each other, we just talked. We really understood each other. It was so nice. I felt like we were getting to know each other so well. And I loved every minute of our time together. It always felt too short, but I dared not go longer, for fear that they would find out I wasn't *just* meeting a friend. I was certain we were destined to be together. If he would just see the light. I'd tried approaching the subject before multiple times, but he would always immediately change the subject. Then one day, he just came out with it.

"I don't like it when you talk about all that Jesus crap. It never did anyone any good. I don't know why you stick with it! Your parents died for believing those crazy stories." I froze and stared at him. "Because it's true. It's not just crazy stories. They're real." "Well, I don't know how anyone could believe they're real if their parents were killed for believing it." "The Bible said there would be persecution. That many would prove their faith with their death." "That's stupid! If your god is so loving as you say he is, why would he let the people who believe in him die?" I thought for a moment. I'd never really thought about that before. "I'll have to get back to you on that one." Anthony frowned. "It's because he's not there! Because it just doesn't work that way. The authorities looked into it when they were building the dome cities. It's so unlikely that any of that happened. It's downright impossible that all of it could." "That's what faith is, Anthony. Believing even when it seems impossible. Trusting even when you can't see. Don't you understand?" "No, not at all. Besides, you're the only one of those Jesus freaks who have treated my family right. You wanna know why we moved to Ring Three?" I frowned. "Weren't your parents' jobs moved?" "That's what we said, but it was really because a Christian coworker kept forcing her beliefs on Mom. and when she wouldn't take it anymore, she filed a complaint. Well, that woman had done nothing wrong, ever. Even when she had been close to bursting because of how pregnant she was. So, they ignored the complaint. Then the next time the woman came at Mom, Mom told her exactly what she thought of her. That's when they fired her. And she couldn't get a job at any of the other salons in Ring One. That's why we moved. That woman had alienated her among all the salons in Ring One." "That's horrible, Anthony. I'm so sorry." He smirked. "I'm not. If it hadn't happened, I wouldn't have met you." He took me into his arms, brushing his hands down the backs of my arms. I smiled dreamily, then I frowned. "It's still not how a Christian should act. It's a poor example of Christ and His love." He chuckled and shook his head. "Someday I'll get you to understand." I shook my head fiercely. "Nothing will dissuade me. I can't be unconvinced of the truth of what I believe." "Nora, I don't want to talk about this anymore." I sighed and nodded. "Okay, but if you could? What was the woman's name? Do you know?" "Oh yes, I'll never forget. Mom complained about her all the time. Kate Brenwood." My stomach clenched. I felt sick. "What? Do you know her?" I nodded solemnly. "A little." More than a little, but why should he know that? He scoffed. "Just ditch her then." My eyes went wide. "What?" "Ghost her. Pretend she doesn't exist. She's dead to you." "B-but she's my friend, Anthony!" "Do you care anything for me, Nora?" I brushed his cheek with my hand. "You know I do." "Then if you truly care about me, then you'll never talk to that woman again, if you can help it." "And if I choose not to?" He chuckled. "Look, Nora, I don't want to fight, but if you're going to continue talking to such an awful person, then out of love for my family, I'm done." My heart stopped. I couldn't lose Anthony! But I couldn't explain to him that she and her husband were the leaders of the underground church I was staying at. That it would be very difficult to avoid her. There were many occasions when I talked to her, even though it wasn't necessary. It was so nice to chat with a motherly figure. Though no one could replace Mom, Kate was great. But I couldn't lose Anthony! "Okay, I won't talk to her anymore." He smiled. "I knew you

71

would make the right choice." He took my face in his hands and kissed my forehead. I smiled weakly. My stomach twisted. I felt like I would throw up. And then I did. Right on the floor. Great. Just great. The old, beautiful rug in the living room now sported a vomit stain, as if a wild party had taken place there. "Woah, woah, woah, you okay, Nora?" "Yeah." I sat down. "I should go." "You sure? Maybe you should come home with me." I shook my head. "No, I can't do that. I need to go home." I stood up. "See you next week, Anthony." I started to walk away. "Wait." I turned around. "What?" "Can I see you sooner than that? I want to take you out for dinner." I sighed. "Fine. I'll see what I can do." He smiled. "Thank you. How's Saturday?" I nodded. "Okay." "Bye, Nora." "Bye, Anthony."

"You look terrible. What happened?" I sat down on my cot. Matthew was sitting on his cot, studying. "Oh, the usual." I answered brightly. "Oh yeah? Then what's with the sour expression on your face?" "Oh, I just felt sick for some reason. Completely unrelated." "Oh, that so?" "Yeah, it's going pretty great, actually. They're very interested in what I have to say. So interested, in fact, that they've asked that we meet again on Saturday." "Oh, nice. Now, when are you going to tell me who this friend is?" "I told you; you wouldn't know him." "*Him*?!" I blushed. Oh gosh. How could I slip like that? "The friend you're meeting is a *guy*?!" "Didn't I tell you?" He spluttered. "What?! No! You haven't told me anything about the person you're meeting!" I shrugged. "Oh. Well, it's okay. He's very nice. You'd like him." He rubbed the back of his neck, then looked at me. "It's that Merrick guy, isn't it?" My face betrayed me. "Elnora, that's so stupid! That boy just wants to milk you for all you're worth and then leave you stranded. Remember what Serah said about him?" "Serah is his younger sister. You shouldn't believe anything she says." "You're being lied to, Elnora." "You're just being overprotective! Anthony loves me!" "Has he told you that?" "No, but I'm sure he will soon." "If you think he will, he probably will as soon as you give him *everything*." "I've already told him I won't be. I set boundaries from the start." "If he actually agreed to that, he was already thinking of how he could get you." "You're crazy." "You're not allowed to see him again. I forbid it!" "You're not Dad! You can't tell me what I can't do!" "Oh yeah, well, if I have anything to do with it, you're never seeing him again. How could you deceive me like this?" "Because I knew you'd react like this! You don't understand!" "Oh, I understand plenty! You lied to me because you were hoping you could convert a boy that you like and surprise me with it to show how grown up you are." I groaned. "Fine! You caught me! Big deal! You still can't make me stay here! I can do what I want!" A tense silence hung between us before Matthew's moan signaled his exit. I smirked. I felt like I handled that well. But the sickness in my stomach let me know it was still there, and it was worse now. What had I done? First, I'd agreed never to speak to Kate again, and now Matthew would never trust me again. I sank onto my cot and cried.

I told Jared my friend wanted to meet me on Saturday. But Matthew had already spoken with him. He told me I would not be meeting with my friend anymore. Just for my safety. But I knew it was because of whatever Matthew told him. He told me I could write a letter, and someone would leave it in Harminny House for him. So, I did. I explained that Matthew had found out that I was meeting with him, and he had been quick to keep me from meeting him again. I knew Anthony would be upset. How could he not be? I gave it to Jared, making it a point not to even make eye contact with Kate. Jared thanked me and assured me he would make sure my friend got it.

Matthew didn't speak to me for a couple of days. Not that I minded. I was mad too. I didn't want to talk to him either. But when he finally spoke to me at lunch one day, I was surprised. "Do you talk to Cal much?" What in the world? "No, not really. Why?" He thought for a moment. "Well, I don't know. I think you should." I stared at him, trying to discern what he wanted me to do. "Why?" "Oh, I just think you two would get along well." I rolled my eyes. "I will not let go of Anthony that quickly, Matthew. So back off." "It's not for you. It's for him." "Why?" "Stop asking that, Elnora. Just talk to him at training tomorrow." I groaned. "Fine. But I hope you don't expect me to fall for him because I won't." "Fine with me."

"Hey." Cal looked up from where he was stretching on the floor. He smiled and stood up. "Hey! What's up?" "Your dad has me sparring with Amy later.

74

Can you give me some pointers?" "Who have you sparred with before?" "They've been having me spar Miriam to start with." "Okay." He thought for a moment. "Amy is all offense." I giggled. "I know, not surprising," he added with a smirk. "Go for the stomach. She doesn't protect it very well." "Got it. Thanks." I stretched with him. "Your family lives in Ring Three, right?" "Yep." "You would have to go to the high school then, right?" "Yeah." "How come I never saw you?" He shrugged. "I saw you." "You did?" "Yeah, it was hard to miss you with that bodyguard of a brother. You hung out with Jennifer Dillon, right?" I nodded. "Yeah." Oh, how I missed Jenn! "Have you seen her since..." I shook my head. "I haven't." "Oh. Dad said you were meeting with someone on Tuesdays. I thought it was her." "No, it was-uh, someone else." He didn't reply. "But I'm not meeting with them anymore." "Oh, why?" "Matthew doesn't think it's wise. Thinks I could get hurt." He didn't respond. We stretched in silence.

"Mox, Pip!" Amy and I came over to the sparring floor. Flat mats covered it to make it softer to fall on. "Ready?" We shook hands and stood at the ready. "Fight!" Amy charged and grabbed me. She flipped me onto my back. I grabbed her around the waist and stood up. I punched her in the stomach. She fell back. I held her down. She fought back, but I won. "Winner: Elnora!" I sat back and helped Amy sit up. "Nice job there, Elnora," she said. "Thanks, you were a good challenge." "Not enough, it seems. You had me down in five seconds." I laughed. Michael put a hand on my shoulder. "Well done." "Thanks." Even Matthew clapped for me.

"I could help you." I whipped around to face Cal. Fresh from a shower, I had just entered the cafeteria. "With what?" "Your friend. I can help you see them." I sighed. "I already told you I can't, Cal." "You can, I can help you." "What do we do then?" "I'll take you. We'll tell Matthew that we're going out. Which we would be. Just not in the way he'll think." "Really? You'll take me to Harminny House?" He nodded. "Wow, Cal, that would be great!" I hugged him. "That's so kind of you! I'll tell Matthew."

I entered our apartment. Matthew sat reading something by a man named C. S. Lewis called *The Screwtape Letters.* "Cal's taking me out Saturday evening," I told him. "Really? That was fast. He must really like you." I frowned. "Is that what you were planning the whole time?" He smiled. "No. Not really, I mean. I just knew he liked you." Oh, no. Cal liked me?! "How could you tell?" Matthew chuckled. "He can't keep his eyes off you." My heart dropped. This was bad. Cal was taking me to meet my friend whom I had been sharing the Gospel with. What he didn't know was that "friend" was Anthony, and that I was going out with him. Matthew had a puzzled expression. "Is something wrong?" I smiled and shook my head. "Nope! I was just thinking, I couldn't remember him from school at all, but we attended the same school.

76

He's the same age as you. So, you should've had all the same classes." "Well, your bubble was rather small, Elnora." I shrugged. "I guess that's true. But how come you two never hung out?" Matthew thought for a moment. "I tried approaching him a couple times, but he just always seemed distracted. I know all the girls in my grade were going after him. I mean, it's hard not to see why. He's jacked, just like his dad." I groaned. "You complained about Anthony, but Cal sounds no different." Matthew laughed. "Oh, sorry, forgot to mention, he's never actually gone out with any of them. Doesn't give them any attention, but they pursue anyway." I sighed. "Well, that makes me feel better. I just thought you'd like to know that he and I are going out." "Thank you. I'm very glad to know."

"Hey, Elnora!" I panicked. It was Kate! I pretended not to hear her and walked toward the apartment. She tapped my shoulder. Oh no! I turned around. "Hey!" "Oh, hi!" "You haven't come by to chat in a few days. Is everything okay?" I nodded. "Yeah, I'm good. Everything's going well." She nodded. "Okay, good! Would you like to come by this afternoon?" I panicked. "Oh, I'm so sorry, but I can't. I'm busy." "Oh, what are you doing?" Ugh, what could I tell her? "Meeting with Diana!" She frowned. "I thought Diana worked in the afternoons?" "She had the day off." "Oh, I see. Well, I hope you have fun!" "Yeah, thanks! I'd better get going!" I walked away. Ugh, that was so awkward! And that was just the first time I had failed to avoid her. How could I do this? Well, maybe Anthony would accept Jesus soon? Yeah! Surely that was it! The Bible says God won't give you more than you can handle. I can handle this! It'll be fine! Maybe tonight would be a breakthrough with Anthony! I prayed it would be so.

"Ready to go?" Cal asked. I nodded. "Yep! Let's go!" He looked me up and down. "You look lovely," he said. I felt myself blush. "Thank you, Cal. You should thank Miriam. When she heard from your mom that we were going out, she offered to get a dress for me. He smiled. "I'll do that." He opened the hatch, then we climbed the ladder. It was true. Kendra told Miriam about Cal and my date; Miriam then asked if I had a nice dress for it. When I had told her I didn't, she said she had the perfect dress for me if I liked it. I had told her she didn't have to. But she brought it to the Bible teaching that evening. It was truly perfect. It was white with slightly puffed long sleeves, an ankle-length skirt, and orange, pink, and lavender flowers sprinkled over it. I braided my hair into a circle on the back of my head. All the girls who had come through the bathroom said I was an absolute vision. Amy particularly had gushed. Even Matthew had complimented me. My date with Cal thrilled him. He thought I was over Anthony. He couldn't have been more wrong.

"Here we are!" "Thank you, Cal. I really appreciate you taking me." I hugged him. "I owe you for this." I climbed up the ladder into Harminny House, grateful for my tights. The basement of Harminny House had never looked sweeter to me. I went into the

78

living room. Sure enough, there Anthony was. He was a little dressed up, too. My letter was in his hand. His face was grim. "Anthony?" He looked up at me. His eyes lit up, and he rushed over to me. "Oh, Nora!" He hugged me. "I was so scared." I nodded. "I know, me too." "If you're here, why did you write the letter?" I swallowed. "Matthew told the people we're staying with, and they made me write it." "I see. And Matthew twisted the story so you couldn't see me anymore." He swore. "Don't say that, Anthony," I pleaded, stroking his arm. "He's just protective, is all. He just doesn't want me to get hurt. Aren't you protective of Serah?" He sighed and nodded. "About Maddie, too, but I've had to turn it off since she moved in with her boyfriend. He's quite the character. Everything he's ever said to her has made me bristle and want to punch him in the face. And she's just gotten so defensive and distant." "I'm sorry. That must be very hard for you." He took a deep breath. "Yes, but I'm dealing with it. Thank you." He cleared his throat. "Anyway, are you ready to go?" I nodded excitedly.

It had been nice to walk in Ring Three again. Anthony took me to a place called Staggio's. It wasn't over-the-top fancy, but it was nice. I'd never been to Staggio's. My family had never gone out to eat. It was extravagant, and the money spent at a restaurant was better spent serving people. Besides, Mom was an amazing cook! We sat down at a candlelit table set for two. A red tablecloth and an ornate golden table runner handsomely decorated the table. A waiter brought a basket of breadsticks. "This place is beautiful, Anthony. Thank you," I said, laying my hand softly on his. "I wanted to do something at least a little nice for my beautiful woman." I felt my face grow warm. But I said nothing. "How long can we be out?" Anthony asked. "I told my friend to come get me if I didn't show up at 9." "Okay, that's not much time, but it's still plenty of time to take a leisurely walk back to Harminny House." His eyebrow quirked. "You don't live there now, do you?" I laughed and shook my head. "No, I don't." "Okay." "I'm so glad my friend was willing to take me to meet you. It was truly godsent." Anthony laughed mockingly. "As if! God had nothing to do with it. You're just a great person who anyone would do a favor for." I sighed. "Anthony, my faith is really important to me. I need you to listen to me." He sighed. "Fine. But don't think you can convert me." My heart sank. Oh God, please help me! I needed to say the right thing that would turn Anthony. I smiled. "Okay."

We talked for a while and ate our food. It was amazingly delicious. And now we were walking back to Harminny House. He had his arm around me as we walked. "Can't you come home with me, Nora? Please!" I smiled sadly and shook my head. "I can't." He hung his head. "I'm sorry." Then suddenly, he pulled me in front of him and kissed me. I'd never felt anything like I felt then. I felt like I was in a distant dream, and just like a dream, when you could have an entire life in just a few hours, it felt like forever before he pulled back. My emotions reeled. Part of me wanted to grab him and kiss him again. Another part of me wanted to flee from Anthony and these bewildering feelings. But he settled me back beside him, an arm around my shoulders as before. When we got back to Harminny House, I didn't wish to part from him. He kissed me quickly and hugged me. "Same time on Tuesday. We'll go see a movie." "A movie? I can't." "Why not?" I shook my head. "There's so much unnecessary filth in movies." "I'll check them out. I'll make sure it's a movie you'll be okay with, or we'll just go for a walk around the Ring." "Okay." "Great. See you then, Nora." "Bye."

"How'd it go?" My mind panicked. That's right! "It went so great, Cal!" "That's awesome!" "Seriously, Cal, what can I do for you?" He played with his fingers and stared at the floor. It was so strange to see such a tall, strong young man feeling so awkward. "Well, you see, I was wondering if we could, maybe, you know, actually go out on a date?" I felt the color leave my face. "What?" "It's fine! It's fine! I didn't think you liked me, anyway." We started walking. How could I handle this? I couldn't reveal my deception. It would mess up everything. "No, no, no! Let's go out!" I took his hands in mine. "How's Monday?" He shook his head and smiled. "It's okay, Elnora. You don't have to pretend you have feelings for me just to spare me mine." "No, I want to go out!" He looked at me strangely. "You do?" Hope flickered in his eyes. I nodded. "Of course, I do! You're great!" He sighed and shook his head. I had to convince him. I threw my arms around his neck and kissed him. He was surprised at first, but then he wrapped his arms around my back, pulling me closer. Panic zapped through me. I pulled back and smiled. He still seemed nervous but agreed. "Okay, we'll go out on Monday." I clapped. "Yay!"

We continued walking down to GIOR. How long had Cal liked me? I couldn't believe I'd kissed him. Though he had thought I didn't like him, it certainly couldn't be denied now. And now I was going on a date with him! But it would be okay. It was just one date. It would be just fine. I could just act super weird so he would stop liking me, and he wouldn't want to go out again. I just hoped Anthony wouldn't somehow discover us.

CHAPTER EIGHT

"Wow! It must've gone really well if you're going out with him again on Monday," Matthew said with a smirk. I sighed dreamily, reminiscing about Anthony's kiss. "Yes, it was wonderful. I couldn't be happier. Thank you, Matthew." I hugged him. It was the next morning, and I had just told Matthew extensively about our date. You know. The one with Cal. The one that never happened. "I'm glad to hear it, Elnora. I was very concerned when I found out you were seeing Anthony. I'm glad to see you've moved on. Anthony would've really hurt you." I smiled, the guilt of my deception gnawing at my stomach. "Did he ever ask you for anything after you'd already told him no?" Last night alone, Anthony had pleaded for me to come home with him. But it was only to protect me. Because he cares so much for me. I shook my head. "No. He never did." He put his hands on my shoulders. "I'm sure he would've soon then. Look, I want you to know I don't do this because I want to ruin your fun. I do this because I'm trying to keep you safe. You're innocent. There are a lot of awful things you don't know about. Things that have been hidden from you for a reason." "I appreciate you wanting to protect me, Matthew, but I know more than you realize. You don't have to be *so* protective." He sighed. "I know. There's only so much that can be hidden from you. Mom and Dad knew you'd find out some things from hanging out with Jenn Dillon. But we were okay with it because you'd never really made a friend before." I smiled. "Thanks. I know you're just being a good brother." I went to the door. "Now come on, we have class."

It had been only six weeks since the execution. Mostly, we stayed distracted, but nights were hard. It was the only time that we couldn't drown our sorrows with school and training. Both of us struggled to hold it together behind closed doors. We were doing our best to hold each other and grieve together, but we could only do so much to help each other while experiencing the same emotions. When we were asking God the same questions. There had been that rough spot between Matthew and me after our parents had died, but after we got the letters from Mom, our relationship had been slowly repairing. Our closeness hadn't yet returned to what it was before our parents died. But we were growing together again. Our classes were going well. Matthew had finally accepted Miss Carrington's teaching style. He admitted he found her exuberance refreshing. Her joy had initially rubbed his grief the wrong way. Where I had found her enthusiasm comforting, he had found it grating. He remained unconvinced by some of her statements, but he mostly lets it go. But sometimes when I ask her questions, Matthew obviously disapproves. Our normal education teacher was nice as well, but not particularly notable. Our lives had become a cycle of numbing our sadness with constant busyness, and right now, that was perfect.

"Feeling up for another mission, Pip?" Michael asked, nudging my elbow. I moved down the cafeteria line. "If you think I can do it." "Absolutely! I know this is new to you, but you've really got a talent for this. I think you can handle it." I smiled. His confidence in me was encouraging. "Okay, when do you want us at the gym?" "Oh, just the normal time. Everyone will be there. I called them in for an emergency mission." "Great! See you then." We parted ways, and I sat next to Elizabeth Brenwood. Suddenly, breakfast didn't seem very appetizing. My stomach fluttered with butterflies. I was nervous, but excited. Mostly because of Cal. I dreaded what people would say about us. Not because it would be bad, but because it would be good. Because everyone would say how cute we are. How perfect we are together. I wanted to scream. I shouldn't have promised him a date. Why had I forced it when he had admitted to not thinking I liked him back? Why had I kissed him to prove to him I liked him when I *didn't*? I felt like I was digging a hole deeper and deeper and deeper, hoping for a spring of water to bubble up, but just getting stuck in mud. Now it would be impossible for Cal not to get hurt.

"Alright, everyone, today's targets are Curtis and Isla Jordan. Curtis was a tailor for *Enchante* Co. His boss, Greg Merrick, turned him in when he found a Bible in his sewing space." My stomach dropped. Anthony's dad had *turned in* a man for being a Christian? Was he aware of Anthony and me? "Isla went to see Greg and begged the authorities to release him. Said her family needed him desperately. She was, in turn, also arrested. The Jordans' kids have been here since Tuesday." I hadn't been here. And when I had, I had been angry and self-absorbed, plotting my next step in my web of manipulations. I had never seen these poor children whose parents someone had brutally taken. I had to do better. How could I do this? I had been associating with the enemy and ignoring those in need. Guilt churned inside me. "They are not in the detention center yet. Currently, they are in the major government building. Being interrogated by specialist Madison Merrick. Who knows what condition they may be in when you get to them? Any questions?" Silence. Nausea flooded me. Maddie? Oh, God, please don't let me run into her! Why had I agreed to this mission? "Great! Now, about the leader of this mission. Miriam, we think you are best suited to lead this mission. You used to work in the main government building, and you know how to administer aid should there be a need." Miriam saluted. "Thank you, sir." "Great! Get ready, everyone. This is much higher stakes than the last mission."

Cal offered to hold on to me again when we got on the helicopter. I told him I would be okay. I thought he might try to kiss me or that he might expect *me* to. The transport took off. We came out of the hole. Again, the cool night air struck me in the face. One learned to appreciate it when you hardly ever went above the surface. I wondered how Matthew felt, having only once come up to the surface since we went underground, and that was for our first mission. I couldn't see him from where he stood with Ezra, behind Cal and Dr. Bennet. I stood with Diana and Miriam.

Amy's voice came over the intercom. "Approaching the Capitol Building." We all moved to the edge. "Ready?" I asked Matthew. "I guess so!" "Come on, team!" Miriam jumped. Followed by Diana, me, Matthew, Dr. Bennet, Ezra, and Cal. We all landed neatly on the balcony of the twenty-second floor of the government building. "Alright. The interrogation level is thirteen." "Think we can take the elevator?" Ezra asked. Miriam gave him a look that shut him up, then she smiled and giggled. "Not today, Ezra." We left the government official's apartment. It was empty at the moment. We ran out into the hallway and did a quick sweep. Diana shot one guard. "Are the cameras turned off, Specs?" Miriam asked, pressing the button on her earpiece. "As soon as you touched down, Mir," Kendra said in our ears. Dr. Bennet paused at the stairwell entrance. "Clear." Miriam ran down the stairs. We all followed her. My legs wanted to give out by the time we reached the thirteenth floor. Miriam scanned the outside before we came out. She shot twice, then gave us a thumbs up. We all moved out into the hallway. "Where's the interrogation room?" Dr. Bennet asked. Miriam walked down the hallway to a metal door. "This way." Ezra and Diana gathered around her as she opened the door. "Clear!" The rest of us ran through. The room was small, but one could not mistake the electric chair in one corner of the room. In another tank were snakes. Many kinds of needles, blades, and such hung on the back wall. The government tortured people!? My stomach twisted. "You didn't think the government was this bad, did you?" Diana asked. I turned to her. "I had no idea they were so cruel." "Torturing people into giving up information about GIOR?" She shook her head. "It's one of their favorite hobbies." I shuddered. My stomach twisted. Why would anyone inflict this on someone else? "I found Curtis!" Cal called from the other room. We all rushed in. A light-brown haired man, his face haggard, was slumped within a cell. He raised his gaze when we entered. He sat up straight and kicked his legs. "*No! Leave me alone! Please!*" "Woah, woah, woah, it's okay, Curtis," Miriam said. Diana unlocked the cell door and slid it open. Miriam went in and knelt in front of Curtis. "I'm Miriam Longbourne. We're from GIOR. We're here to rescue you and Isla." "How are the kids?" She smiled. "They're well, sir. We have them underground with us." He sighed in relief. "Oh, thank, God!" Diana unlocked his cuffs. He massaged his wrists. "Do you have any wounds that need to be dressed? I'm a nurse," Miriam asked him. He shook his head. "Nothing on the outside other than bruises. But I feel like I've taken enough beatings for two lifetimes." "We'll take you back to GIOR. We just need to find Isla. Do you know where they're keeping her?" His eyes turned panicky. "They took her! I don't know where, but they took her!" "We're about to have company," Ezra called from the main room. We all lifted our guns. The door opened. "Hands up where I can see them," Dr. Bennet barked. "Wow, we got an entire party here, don't we?" a familiar voice said smoothly. Those of us in the containment room moved into the main area. I gasped.

Oh, no. I tried to hide behind Cal, grabbing his arm. He glanced back at me with a reassuring smile. He put his hand on mine. The woman looked in my direction and grinned maliciously. "Oh, how nice to see you again, Elnora. Does my brother know you're doing this?" "What is she talking about?" Cal asked me. I felt my cheeks grow red. "What's the matter? Haven't you told everyone about your boyfriend?" "Boyfriend? What is she talking about, Pip?" Ezra asked. "Back off, Maddie," Matthew said. "It's over between her and Anthony." She frowned. "Oh, really?" She asked with mock surprise. "Then how come when I called him last night, he told me he'd just taken her out on a date? They had their first kiss, too, as I recall from our conversation." "Pip, what is she talking about?" Cal asked. "There's no time for this," Diana said. She shot one of Maddie's guards. Doc shot the other. "Where's Isla?" Ezra asked. She smirked. She's in the other room. I doubt you'll find anything worth rescuing, though. My heart thumped. Dr. Bennet, Diana, and Matthew ran past her and into the other room. "Twick, come over here!" Cal and I kept Maddie at gunpoint while Ezra went to help Miriam. "Take Curtis up to the helicopter. Cal, go with him to protect him if he needs it." Cal nodded and ran out with Ezra, who carried Curtis on his back. Miriam came and took Cal's place. "Well, this is fun," Maddie said, a smirk on her face. "Mir!" Dr. Bennet carried in a limp body. "I checked her pulse. It's faint, but it's still there." He laid her in front of her. She knelt in front of her and unhooked the med kit from her belt. "More guards are coming!" Diana called from the hallway. "I need backup!" Matthew and I rushed over. Miriam

89

groaned. "I can't help her while we're here. We just have to pray that she'll still be alive when we get back to base." She put away her med kit, and Dr. Bennet picked her up. "Di, deal with her, please," Miriam ordered. "On it." She loaded a blue dart into her pistol and shot Maddie. Putting it away with a twirl, she said with a smirk, "She'll have a headache in the morning." Matthew shot a guard. "Come on, let's get out of here!" We ran up the stairs. The guards chased after us. Dr. Bennet slumped on the ground. Someone had shot him. "Not now, Doc!" Diana and Matthew put his arms around them while I shot at more guards. "Come on!" When we reached the top floor, Cal was waiting for us. "Doc got shot," Diana explained. Cal took him. Dr. Bennet groaned in pain. Diana and I watched his back as we climbed back up the stairs. We reached the top. Everyone else was on the helicopter. "Come on!" Cal jumped in. Diana yelped and fell to the ground. "Di!" I shot another guard as I ran to defend her. I knew I couldn't pick her up. Cal came to get her. "Come on!" We jumped on the helicopter and flew away. My breath came out in gasps. We had barely escaped from the guards, but I knew there would be no escaping what would happen when we returned to GIOR.

CHAPTER NINE

I panted, adrenaline still coursing through me as we flew away. "You okay?" Matthew asked. I nodded. "Doc and Diana got shot, though." "Descending," Amy said over the intercom. The transport lowered. GIOR medical staff treated Curtis, Isla, Dr. Bennet, and Diana upon our return. "Good work, team," Michael said. "That was a tough mission. Go on and get cleaned up, then rest up. Tomorrow is a new day." Matthew and I started to walk away. I almost ran in my desperate attempt to flee. "Elnora, can I talk to you?" My heart dropped. It was Cal. I sighed and turned to him. "Yeah." I followed him into the corner, away from everyone. His face was pale; his body was tense. "What was that woman talking about? She obviously knew you. She could've been lying, but from your reaction, I don't think she was. Can you explain?" I sighed. "Her name is Madison Merrick. She lives in Ring One, but her family had just moved next door before Matthew and I came underground." "And why was she talking about her brother and you going on a date last night?" I stared at the floor. "Because we did." Shame filled me to the brim. I felt nauseous and wanted to run away. "For how long?" "Pretty much since Matthew and I moved down here. He's the friend I've been meeting with. His name is Anthony. And I'm genuinely sharing the Gospel with him! But that's not all it's been. We went on a date last night, and we *did* have our first kiss." I couldn't bring myself to look at Cal. I fought tears of shame. "You tricked me." I nodded. "Yes." "Then you lied to me and made me think you actually had feelings for me. Even when I didn't think you did! You just kissed me to make me think you did! Do you know how messed up that is?" I felt my face grow warm. "I know, I know, I'm sorry." "Sorry doesn't even begin to cover it." Cal stormed away. The tears fell freely now. What had I done? How could I have done this to such a kind person who cared so much about me?

"Care to explain what that was about, Elnora?" Matthew stood in our hut facing me, his arms crossed, his face serious. Great! And now I'd have to explain it all over again. "She said you and Anthony went on a date yesterday. Is that true?" "Yes." "But I thought you and Cal went out last night." I shook my head. "That was what we said. He heard I was meeting someone and sharing the Gospel with them, but when I told him you wouldn't let me see him. I told him you were just being overprotective. Because you were! And he said he would take me to see Anthony, and we'd say we were going out." Matthew slid his hand over his face, groaning. "Elnora, didn't you know he likes you?" I paused and felt my face turn red. "N-not at the moment, no." "But you do now?" "Yes, he asked me out when we were walking back...and I kissed him." "What!? If you had just seen Anthony, why would you do that?" "Because the only reason I couldn't like him was because of Anthony! And I couldn't let him know that I'd just been on a date!" Matthew's face was emotionless. "You're a piece of work, aren't you? Just a little temptress, huh? Don't care who gets hurt." The tears threatened to fall again. "I guess so," I said tearfully. He said nothing for a few minutes. "Well, I hope you're happy." Then he left. My heart dropped. That's it? No anger or accusation? Just, 'I hope you're happy.' And somehow...it felt worse. If he were angry, then I'd be able to defend myself, but he was just sad. How could I combat that? I lay on my bed, pressed my face to my pillow, and cried. How could this have gone so horribly? If only I had told the truth from the start. There's no way I would be in this mess. But, then again, I wouldn't have gone to meet Anthony and none of the wonderful things with him would've happened either. Why did this have to happen? How could I have been so stupid?

Matthew let me go see Anthony on Tuesday, having given up fighting me. Amy brought me to Harminny House. She was the only one who wasn't mad at me because she didn't know what had happened. Apparently, no one had told her. And she was so oblivious that she hadn't noticed the obvious tension between Cal, Matthew, and me. I climbed up. Anthony stood in the living room like he always did, waiting for me. I ran to hug him. He just stood there stiffly. Something was wrong. I looked up at him. "What's wrong?" "Maddie said she saw you on Sunday, in the government building, with a bunch of those Christian terrorists that have been causing problems everywhere. You helped them take two prisoners." She told him? Of course she did. As if I didn't have enough problems. "Is it true?" I could hear the devastation in his voice. I wanted to cry. "Yes," I answered. Tears threatening to fall. I hugged him tighter, pressing the side of my face to his chest. "Oh, Anthony, everything is so messed up." He pushed me away. "I'm done." My stomach twisted. "What? What do you mean?" "It's over! You're one of them! I can't be with someone who is part of a group of terrorists." "But we're not terrorists! We rescue people who are falsely imprisoned!" "I don't care what you think you're doing! I'm done! We're done! I can't believe I let myself fall for you!" Tears fell freely now. "No, Anthony, please, don't do this!" He went to the door. "As long as you're a part of that group, there is no us. I don't care what feelings I have for you. They can go away. They've always gone away." He opened the door. "Wait!" "Goodbye, Nora." He slammed it. I sank to the ground and cried.

This couldn't be happening. With all the lies and manipulation I'd said and done to keep Anthony, why would he leave? How could he? I'd given up everything for him! Tears flowed freely down my face. What could I do now? I had nothing back at GIOR. They all hated me. And now Anthony was gone. And it was all my fault. But I couldn't go back to GIOR and just say, 'never mind, everyone! You can stop hating me! It didn't work out!' That was when it occurred to me. There was only one place where I could belong, only one place where I was wanted. And I wanted to be wanted so badly. And maybe if I went there, Anthony would take me back.

I entered our apartment. Matthew was studying, as per usual. "You're back early," he said matter-of-factly. I said nothing. I started packing my backpack with my things. "What's going on?" "I'm leaving." He set his book down. "What do you mean, you're leaving? Where are you going?" "I don't belong here. Everyone hates me after what I did to Cal. So, I'm leaving." He stood. "Don't do that. Please, Elnora. It'll blow off soon." I turned to him. "No, it won't. I can't even look at Cal without thinking about what I did to him." I zipped up my backpack and slung it over my shoulder. "It's better for everyone if I go." "That's not true." I hugged him. "Please, don't go." "Goodbye, Matthew." "Mom said to stick together!" "Well, Mom wasn't betting on me becoming 'a little temptress' now, did she?" "Things will get better. You're human. Everyone makes mistakes. Just...don't leave." "I have to." I approached the door. "Stay safe, big brother."

I didn't bother telling anyone; I knew the passcode. Nobody needed to accompany me. I didn't need protection when I was just a hindrance. I climbed back into Harminny House. The basement looked dismal and bleak now, reflecting my emotions perfectly. I entered the living room. The stain was still there from when I'd gotten sick. I should've cleaned it before I left that day. I could've shown at least that much respect for one of Midas' historical monuments, run down as it may be. Great! Just add more guilt to the pile. I stepped outside. The afternoon sun shone down. I walked past my old house. I didn't belong there either. The innocent girl who had grown up there was gone. Now I was just...what? Things had changed so much, I didn't even know who I was anymore. I got on the subway which took me to the central station where I boarded the train to Ring Five. It took an hour and a half to get there as the trains go in a spiral around the rings. There's no other train in Ring Five. I walked to Winter Street, a street I only recognized from important papers. It's dark when I reach the small, dilapidated house. I knocked on the door. I heard an assortment of cussing as someone came to the door. It opened. A woman with long blonde hair and fascinating dark blue eyes stood before me, smoking a cigarette. "Who are you? This is a dangerous part of town. You should go back where you came from before you get hurt." "I'm Elnora, Aunt Elspeth." Her face lit up. "Elnora!" She hugged me. "What are you doing here? I'm so happy to see you're okay! I saw what happened to your parents. I'm so sorry. Did you get my letter?" "I was staying with some friends after Mom and Dad died, but...they're not my friends anymore." "Oh, you poor thing. Come in! Come in! I'll get my guest room set up for you! It's all dusty cause I haven't had someone stay with me in years. So, I apologize." I came inside and set down my backpack. The house was messy and reeked of stale smoke and alcohol, just like Aunt Elspeth. But it was a decent place. It just needed to be cleaned up and freshened. "Are you hungry? I can whip something up for you real quick." "No, that's alright. Thank you." I couldn't have eaten anything

96

even if I tried. She led me up the stairs to the second floor. There were two bedrooms and a bathroom. Aunt Elspeth led me into the one on the right. "You can stay here. I'll get some sheets from the bathroom real quick." I set down my backpack on the floor. The unadorned room mirrored the house's deterioration. The walls showed cracks, and bubbles appeared on the ceiling, along with some cracks in a corner. The bed was old, and the frame was falling apart. She returned with a pile of sheets. "Here we go." She sloppily spread the sheet over the bed. I put a hand on it. "Here. I'll take care of it, Aunt Elspeth." She stood up. She smiled shyly. "Oh, okay. Well, I-I'll just be downstairs if you need anything." "Thank you." She left, and I made the bed. Well, this was life in Ring Five, I guessed. Other than Ring Six, it was the poorest section of Midas. I couldn't imagine how it got worse in Ring Six. But I'd have to get used to it. This would be my life now. And this was a great place to stay, too. I could talk to Aunt Elspeth. Maybe I could even get her to come back to her faith? I would go see Anthony first thing tomorrow. Oh. Wait. He had school. I might spend the morning at Ring Three, then visit him at school that afternoon. I could see Jenn too! Oh! This was all going to be so great! I thanked God for this great opportunity to tell people about Him before I fell asleep.

CHAPTER TEN

Though it was easy to fall asleep, it was hard to stay that way. The sheets were scratchy, and the mattress was hard. I wanted so badly to sleep, but my mind kept going back to GIOR, to Matthew, Kate, Cal, and all the other people I'd let down. It was tormenting. But when I finally fell asleep, it felt like five minutes before the sun was trying to burst through the curtains at the window. I donned a white blouse and a pink skirt, then braided my hair into a bun. I put on my gray sneakers and went downstairs. Aunt Elspeth lay unconscious on the couch, a bottle in her hand. I sighed, then rummaged through the kitchen for a box of cereal. There was *nothing*! No bread, eggs, milk, anything! What did Aunt Elspeth live on? Well, while I waited for school to be out, I could drop by the house, get my babysitting money, and buy some groceries. I left a note on the fridge for Aunt Elspeth telling her where I was going and when I'd be back, so she wouldn't worry. I grabbed my backpack and left.

I took the train to Ring Three. My stomach was growling violently after that, so I decided to run over to my old house to get my money for food. I took the small subway to Station Axwell and walked to my house. The door was unlocked. I went inside, and I wanted to cry as I entered the kitchen. Oh! It was home! It didn't feel like home, but part of my soul still felt like I belonged here. I went up to my old room. It was so clean and white and neat, just like I'd always kept it. I rummaged through my closet and dresser until I found three outfits that I liked, then took all the cash out of the little shoebox on my dresser. I put them in my backpack and left.

I ate breakfast at a newly opened bakery called Berries & Bluebells. It was such a sweet little spot. The walls were painted in baby blue and every table decorated with fresh cut flowers. I got two of their signature blueberries and cream muffins and settled myself at a corner table to eat while I put together a grocery list. They were the best blueberry muffins I'd ever tasted. Mom had been a great cook, but baking was another story. I only remember two times that she'd ever made a cake, and both had literally ended up in flames. I chuckled at the memories, catching myself by surprise. That was the first time I'd thought of Mom and didn't feel like I'd been stabbed in the heart. The grief was softening, and I was learning to smile again.

I went grocery shopping keeping a careful count of the cost but still buying enough for a week or even two for me and Aunt Elspeth. After that, I went to the library, not one I'd visited before, and sat outside the high school, reading a book. When school let out, a crowd of kids came rushing out. And, of course, the first person I saw was Cal. He saw me too. I wanted to hide in the bushes behind me. "Oh, God, please, don't let him see me," I whispered under my breath. I turned away and pretended to be reading my book. "Elnora?" Oh, no... I closed my book and turned to face him, forcing a smile on my face. "Hey, Cal." "What are you doing here?" "I'm waiting for a friend." "Who? Anthony?" "Since you asked, yes." "You could still come back, Elnora. We need you." "No, you don't. You have Matthew. He's all you need. I don't belong there. Everyone hates me anyway." "I don't hate you." "Well, you should. I treated you the worst of everyone. That's why everyone hates me. Because of what I did to you." "But I don't hate you." "Only because the Bible says you shouldn't. I'm sure deep down you think I'm the worst person to ever exist." "I don't think that. You're my friend." "Friends can be terrible people too." I turned away from him, tears pricking at my eyes. "Just leave me alone, Cal." His eyes darkened. "Okay. Uh, I guess I'll see you later then." He walked away. I sighed. Why, God? Why of all the students who could have approached me after school did it have to be Cal? I scanned the crowd for a known face. Then I spotted him. Anthony. I weaved through the crowd to him. He saw me and stopped. "Hi," I said, my face warm with embarrassment. His face was as stern and unmoving as a mountain. "Hi. What do you want?" "I want to try again." He shook his head. "No." He pushed through the crowd some more. I grabbed his arm. "But wait, Anthony! Please. I've left them." "How do I know you're not lying to me?" I hung my head, tears threatening to spill once again. "Please, can't we just go sit down and get something to eat? I want to explain." He thought for a moment, then sighed. "Fine.

But I need to go get Serah first." "Can I come with you?" "No." "Oh...okay." I smiled. "I'll-uh meet you at Staggio's then." "Yep." He walked away towards the middle school. I took a breath. Well, that was...something. He obviously didn't want to have anything to do with me, but- "Elnora!" I knew that voice. I turned towards the crowd. "Jenn!" My friend wove through the crowd until she reached me and gave me a big hug. She clung to me as if I were her life preserver. Her words came out in sobs, "I was so scared, Elnora. After what happened to your parents, I went to your house, but you weren't there. I was scared something awful had happened to you, and, oh, I'm so glad you're okay." Tears of joy threatened to fall. She released me and wiped her face, mascara now giving her dark shadows under her eyes. "What are you doing here? Where have you been?" "I stayed with some friends for a while, and now, I'm staying with my aunt in Ring Five." "Your aunt? Why her? I thought she wasn't supposed to see you." "Well, my parents are gone, so Aunt Elspeth is my closest living relative." "But I thought there was a restraining order on her?" "There was. But I chose to go live with her." "What about Matthew?" "Oh, he's still living with our friends. I couldn't live with them anymore. They didn't like me." Jenn's brow furrowed. "Oh, who wouldn't like you?" I shrugged. The pain of leaving was still too fresh. "It doesn't matter, anyway. I'm living with Aunt Elspeth now." "Okay, well, do you wanna come over?" "I'm going out already. But how about tomorrow?" "Okay, yeah, sounds good." She blinked. "Wait, you're going out with someone?" I nodded, and a smile spread across my face. "Yes." "With who?" "Anthony Merrick." Her jaw dropped. "You're going out with *Anthony Merrick*?" "I've been seeing him for more than a month." "Are you serious?" I nodded excitedly. "Yes!" Jenn hugged me again. "Oh my gosh, this is amazing! All the girls have been trying to catch his eye. Cal Castrow is practically last season now." "Really?" "Oh, yeah! Who wouldn't want a total hottie from Ring One?" I laughed. "Alright, well, I'll see you later, Jenn." "Alright, see ya! Don't disappear on me again!" "I won't. I promise."

I waited on a bench outside the restaurant, reading my book. Anthony came around the corner. I waved at him. He jogged over. "Hey." I put my book inside my backpack and stood. "Hey. Are you ready to talk?" "Guess so." "Okay. Come on, let's go inside." We sat down at the same table we had on Saturday. We gave our orders, and then we got down to business.

"I left my friends where I was staying before. I'm not on the Search and Rescue Team anymore. I hope you can forgive me." He thought for a moment, then sighed. "You really love me, don't you?" he asked. "Yes, Anthony. I really do." He just stared, then cleared his throat. "Um, yeah, maybe I was too hasty last night. I'm sorry." I smiled. "There's nothing to forgive." I squeezed his hand. "Are you done with all that faith stuff, finally?" "No, absolutely not. I never will be." "Well, one of us will have to change our opinions. And it's not gonna be me." "We'll see about that." The server brought a basket of breadsticks. We both took

102

one. "So, where are you living now?" "With my aunt in Ring Five." His face paled. "Ring Five? Are you serious? That place is dangerous." I shrugged. "I'm alright." "How come you guys lived in Ring Three and never helped her out?" "Well, you see, she lived in Ring Three all her life. She used to come over a lot when I was little, but then one day, she kidnapped me, and she was arrested. Anyone who's been to jail has to live in Ring Five or Six. To protect the higher citizens. That's the law." "Why did she kidnap you?" "To protect me from my parents' faith. Said she was going to give me a better life." I said nothing for a moment. "She had been drinking a lot, and she'd never drank even a little before then, so it made her mind go a little loopy even when she was sober." "Oh...so why are you living with her?" I shrugged. "I know I'll be welcome there." "You could come home with me?" I chuckled softly and shook my head. "You know I'm not doing that." "Isn't there anywhere else you can stay? "My friend Jenn might offer, but her grandparents already live with her family, so her house is full." I put my hand on his and squeezed reassuringly. "It's alright, Anthony. I'll be safe." He sighed. "Fine, but I don't like it." "I know. I appreciate your concern for me, but I'll be okay."

The rest of the dinner was nice and relaxing. I went back to Aunt Elspeth's house and made her dinner. She inquired regarding my daily activities and whereabouts. I brought home groceries. She was grateful. Once I had tidied up, I let her know I was tired and headed to bed. Something felt off. But how could it? I was where I was supposed to be. Right? Aunt

Elspeth had welcomed me into her home. I could share the Gospel with her. I was back with Anthony. I could keep sharing it with him. And now Jenn and I can hang out again. I could continue sharing it with her, too. Surely it would click for one of them soon. Everything was fine. It was all fine.

The next week consisted mostly of taking care of Aunt Elspeth and making her house livable. She needed a lot of help. It's beyond me how she's survived this long by herself. She particularly needed help in the morning. She always woke up with a massive hangover. Most evenings, she wasn't even home. She told me she had a boyfriend that she went out with. Where they went, she never told me, and I didn't really want to know. It was always a relief to see her collapsed on the couch in the morning.

Ring Five was an interesting place. I'd been to Ring Six with my parents plenty of times. But I'd never been to Ring Five before. Some people appeared frightening, others, frightened. There were those that were here because of what they'd done, and those that were here because there was nowhere better for them. It was almost worse than Ring Six. At least the people there looked out for each other. Here in Ring Five everyone was looking out for one person: themselves.

A peculiar man frequented the train station daily. I quickly concluded that he lived there. Something about him was mysterious and magnetic, but uncertainty and fear made me initially avoid him.

However, about a week after I moved in with Aunt Elspeth, I decided to approach him. I got off the train one afternoon after going to the cafe with Anthony, and he was there, sitting on the bench like he usually was. He wore a tattered poncho, and grime coated him. I fingered the paper bag containing a muffin I hadn't eaten. I had been planning to give it to Aunt Elspeth, but he looked like he hadn't eaten in weeks. I sighed and walked over to him. "Hello," I said with a little wave. He looked up at me. I could see some of his face now as he looked up. His eyes widened in fear. I held out the bag to him. "What is it?" he asked. His voice only confirmed his nervousness. "It's a blueberry muffin from a cafe in Ring Three. You can have it." He stared at me in confusion. "Why would you give me this?" "Oh, I had plenty at the cafe. Please. Take it." I smiled gently. He blinked, then glanced at the paper bag in his hand, then back at me. "Th-thank you," he said. "You're welcome." I patted his shoulder and walked out of the station.

The next day, when I made spaghetti for lunch, I brought him some. Again, his surprise gave way to gratitude. The day after that, I brought him pancakes. I couldn't help but notice his eyes shine at the sight of them. And after that, I brought him grilled chicken and green beans. That was when he decided to talk to me.

"What's your name?" "Elnora," I told him. I left out my last name purposefully. "What's yours?" "Jeffrey. Jeffrey Waterbell. But that doesn't really matter." "It's nice to meet you, Jeffrey." We shook hands. "If you don't mind my asking, don't you have a home to go to?" He nodded. "I do. But the station gives more protection against the elements than it does, so I just stay here." "I'm sorry." He shook his head. "It's not your fault." I sat next to him on the bench. "You don't really belong here in Ring Five," Jeffrey said. "Why do you say that?" "You're not like the rest of the people here. Everyone here is either cold and cutthroat or hiding from all those who are." I shrugged. "I trust God will protect me." His blue eyes looked like they'd pop. "You know God?" I smiled and nodded. Excitement rising within me. "Do you?" He nodded. "I do." I squealed. "This is amazing!" I hugged him, regardless of all the dirt and grime on him. "Oh, it's so nice to meet someone who believes!" I released him and sat back. "I forgot to tell you my last name. It's Rembrick." "A Rembrick? Like Lucas Rembrick?" I nodded. "Yes, he was my father." "He's the one who told me about God!" I felt tears coming to my eyes. "He did?" He nodded. "He came to Ring Five four years ago. I was eighteen and had been living on my own since I was twelve. His words filled me with life. I haven't been the same since." A tear slid down my face. "That's wonderful, Jeffrey." "Do you all live down here now?" I shook my head sadly. "Two months ago, the authorities killed my parents for their faith. I'm living here with my aunt." "I'm so sorry. I know what it's like to suddenly lose your parents. Who is your aunt?" "Elspeth Rembrick, do you know her?" "No, never heard of her." "I suppose that might be best." "Why?" I shrugged, not answering. I looked at the big clock above the station. "Speaking of which, I have to go. She'll be needing me. It was great meeting you, Jeffrey." I left the station. I couldn't believe it! Another believer here in Ring Five. God truly was smiling down on me.

That was an added joy to my life here in Ring Five. It was so wonderful to have a friend who believed. I talked to him almost every day. I brought him lunch, and we would talk while he ate. He was so much like Matthew. It was like having another big brother.

One night, after a date with Anthony, I came off the train, and Jeffrey called me over. "Where did you go today?" he asked. "Oh." I blushed. "My boyfriend lives in Ring Three. I was on a date with him." "Oh, what's his name?" "Anthony Merrick." "Is he a believer?" I shook my head glumly. "Not yet. I talk to him about my faith every time we go out though." "Is he receptive? Do you think he'll convert soon?" For once, I didn't lie. I shook my head. "His family is very against believers. I haven't even seen the rest of his family since we met. Not really, at least. I've seen his older sister, but it was not under good circumstances." "Why do you continue seeing him then?" "I really think I can help him! That's why I'm staying with Aunt Elspeth, too." He shook his head. "Elnora, I think this is all more trouble than it's worth. I think you should go back to your brother and your friends' underground. They need you." I laughed. "No, they don't! They all hate me! They're glad I'm gone!" He shrugged. "I'm not so sure about that." I scoffed. "How would you know? You've never even been there." "I had a dream last night." "About what?" "About you and that underground church. They need you, Elnora. And if you continue ignoring the call, you're going to fall deeper and deeper into sin." "Sin? I'm not sinning! I'm doing what's right and sharing the Gospel with people! That's not true!" I spluttered. "W-what are you even talking about?" "You are sinning in denying the call. And the longer you ignore it, and the longer you continue this relationship, the deeper you will fall, and the harder it will be to climb out." I rolled my eyes. "You don't even know him, Jeffrey. How can you say that?" "Because you're getting angry. You know it in your heart, even though you deny it with your mouth." I groaned. "Look, I gotta go, Jeffrey. Aunt Elspeth is going to need me. See you later." I walked away, fuming. How dare he accuse me?! I was not sinning! I was doing what was right! I was ministering to Anthony and Aunt Elspeth, and even Jenn! Surely one of them would come to believe soon! Jeffrey didn't know anything! I fumed as I walked home. How could he accuse me of something so stupid? I was doing the right thing. Everything I was doing was good! How could it be wrong? I was *not* sinning, and nothing he said could convince me of that.

CHAPTER ELEVEN

The next morning, I came downstairs, dressed in a white blouse and a pale blue pleated skirt. Aunt Elspeth was in the kitchen, fumbling around. "Good morning, Aunt Elspeth," I greeted her. "Good morning, Elnora," she mumbled. I took her arm. "Here, why don't you sit down? I'll get you some coffee and make you breakfast." "That's alright, sweetie. I'm fine," her words went up and down in volume as she spoke. She wasn't fine. "Please? You know how much I love cooking." She sighed. "Okay, okay." She sat down at the small wooden table in front of the kitchen. I whipped up some coffee, eggs, and toast quickly. I sat next to her, and we began eating. "Lucas has been so nice to let you stay with me." I frowned and stared at her, puzzled. "Dad didn't send me here, Aunt Elspeth. He died. I came here myself." "Lucas is dead!? What about Luci?" I sighed. "She's dead too." "What happened to them?" "They were executed. For believing in God." She swore. "That's stupid! Who would kill such nice people just for believing in God?" "The Bible said it would happen. Jesus said there would be persecution and that some would die for their faith." "I remember," she said sadly, gripping her coffee mug. "I just never thought it would happen to Lucas." "I know. None of us did." She didn't say anything else until she finished eating. She was staring at the coffee in her mug when she asked, "Do you believe in God, Elnora?" I nodded. "With all my heart." "Good." Her face twisted and her voice quavered, "I wish I hadn't given it up." She let out a sob and covered her face with her hands.

What? She wished she'd never given up her faith? This was great! I put a hand on her arm. "You can try again. It's not too late." She shook her head. "No, you don't get it. I've done horrible, awful things. Things I could not even dare to mention in front of you." I took her hand. "But the Bible says that it's okay. That you are a new creation in Christ. The past doesn't matter anymore. Just come back to Him." She suddenly looked solemn. "Maybe," she mumbled. "I'll have to think about it." She patted my head. "You're a good girl, Elnora." I smiled. She stood up and started towards the stairs with her cup of coffee. "I think I'll take a nap." "Okay, I'll see you later. Sleep well!" After Aunt Elspeth went upstairs, I wanted to hoot and shout in joy. She wanted to come back to faith! I knew I'd come here for a reason. That's when a, well, more selfish thought came to mind. HA! Take that, Jeffrey! If I *were* sinning, that wouldn't have happened. I was supposed to be here, and he had to be all doom and gloom.

I went to the train station at noon. Jeffrey was in his usual spot. I went and sat next to him. "Hey." I handed him an aluminum-wrapped biscuit sandwich with bacon, egg, and cheese. "Thanks." He took part in it with joy. "You're a great cook, Elnora." I smiled. "Thanks." He didn't apologize for his behavior last night. "My aunt was asking some questions at breakfast. She wants to come back to faith," I said, trying to sound casual. "Oh?" He said. "Yep." Still no apology. I put my backpack on and stood up. "Well, anyway, I gotta go. I'm meeting a friend at the shopping centre in Ring Two." "Okay, see you later! Thanks for breakfast." "Of course, no problem!" I turned towards the train. "See you later, Jeffrey." I got on the train. What was wrong with him? He didn't even apologize! I'd brought him breakfast and proved him wrong! And yet, he acted like nothing had ever happened. Ugh, men! They were so prideful!

It was Saturday, so I met Jenn at Ring Three Shopping Centre. "Hey!" Jenn waved to me from the bench she sat at inside the entrance. "So, where are we gonna go today?" I asked cheerfully, putting an arm through hers. "Oh, I've been thinking, you don't have any dresses, fancy dresses either. And with you dating Anthony, you need at least one really nice dress." I thought for a moment. "But wouldn't that be expensive?" "Pish posh! I know where to go. Come, dearest friend of mine. I will find you a gown fit for a princess." We giggled as we stepped onto the escalator.

Jenn picked three dresses and had me try them on. A short red lace dress came first. It had long, flowy sleeves and a plunging V-neckline. Jenn said it complemented my hair wonderfully and made my eyes pop. But it was uncomfortable, and I felt like it barely covered what was necessary. But I didn't say anything. The second was a lovely soft cerulean; the

111

skirt went down to the floor, but there were no sleeves, and I felt like the dress was a little too much for just a date with Anthony. Jenn agreed. Before heading into the changing room to change into the last dress, something caught my attention. A dress of the palest pink with white petals sprinkled over the thin transparent top skirt. The bodice was modest, though it had lots of ruffles and white petals. "Can I try that one on?" I pointed at the dress. Jenn examined it thoughtfully. "No, it's much too innocent. We don't want you to look like a child. Come on, put this one on." I tried to hide my disappointment. "Okay." I took the dress and went into the changing room. The last dress was black with a silver strap on one shoulder; a silver butterfly graced the left rib of the bodice. It lacked something, despite its casual style and greater modesty compared to the other dresses. When I showed Jenn, she concurred. "I guess black's not really your color. Well, the red one looks absolutely *divine* on you. So, let's get that one!" I wanted to resist, but Jenn knew fashion, so it would probably be okay. The petal pink dress caught my eye repeatedly, from the moment we walked away from that area of the store, through checkout, until we exited the store. But, I supposed, it was just not meant to be. "You have a date with him tonight, don't you?" Jenn asked as we left the store. I nodded. "Yeah." "You should totally wear this! He'll love it." I laughed, trying to hide my discomfort. "Alright, I will." "Yay! You *have* to tell me his reaction!" I heard her stomach growl, and we laughed. "Come on, let's go get some lunch," she said.

That night, I met Anthony at Staggio's. He looked me up and down. A warmth and fire filled his eyes, both gratifying and scary. He kissed me, long and drawn out, right in front of the restaurant. "I'm so glad to see you," he said, rubbing the back of my arms. I giggled. "We saw each other yesterday." "I know, but I miss you every moment I'm not with you." My face grew warm. "You look gorgeous." "Thank you." I looked down at the dress. "Jenn found it." "Well, she did a good job." He kissed me again. I laughed and took his hand. "Come on. I'm hungry."

As we waited for our food to come, we chatted. "Aunt Elspeth said she wants to come back to Christianity," I told him. He smiled inauthentically. "That's great, Nora." "I know, I'm so excited." "You know, I've been thinking. About your friends. The ones you used to stay with." "Oh? What about them?" "You know, maybe I judged them unfairly. Maybe they're not terrorists. I mean, you were with them, and you definitely aren't. Could you maybe tell me about them?" Surprised by the question, I nodded. He was curious. "Well, Amy flew the transport. She's a pilot." "A pilot? Those are few in Midas." "I know! But God is using her. And she's very good at it. She's very energetic and has a temper like a redhead. Not including me, of course. Then there is Ezra, he's a goofball, but he can be serious when he needs to be." Anthony smiled with amusement. "Then there is Diana. She's super tough and serious. She lives in Ring Five, so she's used to a rough environment. Then there is Cal. He's Michael and Kendra's son; those are the leaders. He's..." I thought for a moment and smiled softly. "Kind. Always willing to help anyone. He won't even ask why." "Then there is Dr. Bennet. He's from some other country. He has an accent more refined than anyone in the dome cities. Then there's Miriam. She's sweet and kind. She's a nurse, you know. I've never met anyone so selfless. Then, of course, there's my brother, Matthew. He's well, Matthew." "That's cool, Nora. You know, maybe there's more to it than I realized. Maybe there's some credit to this faith you have." I grinned. "It's the best thing you can ever experience." He laughed. Oh, well, I don't know about that." "Well, it's the best thing I've ever experienced." "Do you think we could meet at the park tomorrow so we can talk more about this?" I nodded. "Yeah! That would be great!" Anthony was curious about my faith, too! This was amazing! I couldn't believe it! It was really happening! The thing I'd been waiting for since I met Anthony. Things really couldn't get better right now. At least...that's what I thought. Part of my heart was strangely homesick for GIOR. Sometimes it even made me sick to my stomach. It was so strange. I'd only lived there for almost two months; it's not like it was home. I should be homesick for the beautiful little house I'd lived in my whole life, not the dingy bomb shelter that I lived in for two months.

I saw Jeffrey upon my return to the station that evening, so I went to talk to him. He smiled when he saw me approaching. "Hey, Elnora. You look chipper." I sat next to him. "Anthony was asking questions tonight! He wants to hear more tomorrow!" Jeffrey's smile shifted. His eyes adopted a weariness. "That's great, Elnora. I'm happy for you." I gave him a proud smile. "See, I told you I was doing the right thing." He sighed. "For your sake, I hope you're right. I just hope that you aren't hurt too much" I scoffed. What a downer! "Don't doubt so much, Jeffrey. You gotta learn to trust God's timing and His plan." He tried to smile, but again, it didn't reach his eyes. "Okay, Elnora." I could tell he still wasn't sure of me. But that was his choice. It's not like I cared what he thought. Just like I didn't care what Matthew thought. I was doing what I was supposed to. There was no denying it. But I had no idea what was about to happen.

CHAPTER TWELVE

Sunday was somehow a reverent day for Aunt Elspeth. She drank less and stayed home all day. Proof that her upbringing still had *some* hold over her conscience. I made biscuits and sausage gravy for breakfast, as well as a pot of coffee. As we sat down, I asked her if I could pray for the food. "Fine," she replied. She bowed her head and folded her hands. I did the same and prayed, "Lord, we thank You for this morning. We thank You that Your son died on Friday and rose on Sunday. We thank You for this food. Please nourish it to our bodies and give us energy for the day ahead. In Jesus' name, Amen." We started eating. Aunt Elspeth sighed. "Elnora, whatever I told you yesterday, don't put all your faith in it." I blinked. "About what?" "About God. About faith." My heart sank. "W-what do you mean?" "I was drunk, Elnora. People say a lot of strange, uncharacteristic things when they're drunk." "But-but, you said you wanted to come back? You were crying about it." "That doesn't matter. Don't believe anything I say when I've been drinking. It's not reliable." She took another bite of her food. "So, you don't regret rejecting faith?" She nodded. "Don't regret it at all. I'm so much happier without all those rules." I frowned. "Really?" "Oh, yeah, definitely. I didn't realize how miserable I had been until I did. Those rules are so oppressive. They don't give you any kind of freedom. I understand you were raised believing that without God you have a hole in your heart. It's not true. They just tell you that, so you don't want to try living without Him. But I'm just fine! I've been just fine without Him! I never needed Him in the first place! It was my faith that got me in trouble, not leaving it." "Oh." She put a hand on mine. "You have a good heart, Elnora. There isn't a bad bone in your body. But you will not convert me. I left the faith, and I'm not coming back. There's nothing you can do to make me regret it. You can believe what you want, but, honestly, your father brainwashed you."

I couldn't believe this. But I thought I had been making progress! How could I have been so wrong? There was no way. I had to be right! She was just in denial. Right? But what could I do? Aunt Elspeth ate the last bite of her food. "Good gravy, sweetie. You cook like your mother." I smiled softly, grateful for the comparison to Mom. "Thanks." "What are your plans for today?" "I shrugged. "I'll just be here. But I'm meeting Anthony at the park near his house in Ring Three tonight, and I'll bring lunch to Jeffrey." Her brow quirked. "Jeffrey?" "Yeah." Then I remembered she'd been drunk when I'd told her about him. She was always at least partially intoxicated. Aunt Elspeth laughed hoarsely. "Don't tell me you're two-timing! You've got more guts than I thought!" I panicked. "No, no, no! I'm not! Jeffrey lives at the train station. He has a home, but it's not very nice. So, he stays there. I always bring him lunch. If I ever have leftovers from dates, I give them to him too." She chuckled softly. "You really are much too good for this world, Elnora. Especially Ring Five." She sat down on the couch and turned on the TV. I sat down next to her with my cup of coffee. She flipped to the news. A picture of Maddie came on the screen. "Government official, Madison Merrick, single-handedly uncovered the identities of multiple people involved in the rebel movement. They were arrested last night with help from the local law enforcement." I choked and hacked. Maddie!? "You alright," Aunt Elspeth asked worriedly. I nodded. "Among those detained was the son of the rebel leaders who were executed three months ago, Matthew Rembrick. He was found in Ring Three with fellow rebel Jared Brenwood." Matthew and Jared were captured!? "Also detained were members of the radical group that have been causing chaos throughout the city: Diana Inkwell and Dr. Darcy Bennet, as well as the radicals' leader, Kendra Castrow. President Xao Min gave a speech this morning at the Capitol announcing the capture of these rebels and their judgment. They will execute them tomorrow morning at ten. The viewing will be mandatory for all citizens..."

My mind tuned out everything else. How did this happen!? How did Maddie find them? She'd only seen us on that one mission. And while she'd recognized Matthew and me, it had been weeks since then. How could she have found them? I rushed up the stairs towards the bathroom, feeling more nauseous by the second. That's when it struck me. *Anthony.* He had asked me a billion questions about GIOR last night!

Specific questions. Oh! What a fool I was! I shouldn't have revealed so much. I had unknowingly helped with the detainment of my friends! After I threw up all my breakfast, I sat on my bed in utter shock. It was all my fault, and yet I could do nothing. I had rejected everyone at GIOR for a boy. The same boy who had used me to get information for his sister. What a mess I'd made! Tears of hopelessness fell down my face. I'd failed everyone. Matthew, Cal, Amy, Kate, Dad, Mom, even God. I had wanted to help the people I cared about. To do God's work and change Midas forever, one person at a time. And instead, I had betrayed everyone I loved by trying to take God's responsibilities into my hands. "I'm sorry, Mom," I said with a sob. "I failed you. I compromised my morals to bring the light to someone, and everything went horribly wrong. I followed my heart and called it God, and now this happened. I'm so sorry!" "Elnora!" Aunt Elspeth called my name. "You have a guest! A very handsome one at that!" Fury surged through me. Anthony *dared* to come visit me now! He had never deigned to come to Ring Five before. I heard quiet voices, then someone climbing up the stairs. Someone knocked on my bedroom door. "Go away!" The door opened. It wasn't Anthony, but Jeffrey! "What do you want?" I asked him. "Gonna gloat about how right you were?" He shook his head. "Well, what is it then? Can't you just leave me alone?" "Elnora, I'm not judging you. I came here to encourage you." "Encourage me? Now?" "Yes. I know you feel lost and hopeless, but you have to get up. Even now, there is *still* hope." "How? They're all going to be executed tomorrow, and it's my fault.

Anthony used me to get information for his sister. He wasn't interested in my faith at all!" "I know. But God has a plan." "I know! He always does! My parents have told me that my whole life! Doesn't make me any less of a screw up!" "He wants to use you in His plan. He chose you." "Don't you start! How could He use me now!? I've messed up so enormously. I can't be trusted to do anything." "He knows your heart. You want to save the world. But Jesus already did. You can't have the weight of the world on your shoulders, but He can. You need to give the weight to Him and just do what He has chosen you to do." "Like what? Make spaghetti and take it to them and say, 'So sorry I betrayed you all. Here's your last meal'." "No. You're going to save them." I blinked. "S-save them? But how?" "Go back to GIOR." "What? But how can I? I betrayed all of them!" "God will help you. Just trust Him. Go back." I thought for a moment. "You're saying I can make things right?" He nodded. "You have been chosen, Elnora Rembrick. For such a time as this. Now rise and take hold of what God has given you." Jeffrey's words struck something within me. I felt renewed, determined. I knew what I had to do. It would be hard, but if God wanted me to do it, I would do it faithfully. I stood up. "I'll do it." "Good." "Will you come with me?" He shook his head. "I cannot." "But why?" He crossed his arms and looked away. "I don't belong there." "Of course you do. You're a Christian, just like the rest of them." He said nothing. "Please, Jeffrey?" He shook his head. "Not today, Elnora." And just as quickly he had come, he was gone.

I changed into a more practical outfit for venturing through the sewers. Jeans and a black t-shirt. I packed my things and hurried down the stairs. Aunt Elspeth stood wobbling, a bottle in her hand. "Where are you going, Elnora? I thought you weren't leaving until tonight.". "Thank you for hosting me, Aunt Elspeth. But I need to go. I've stayed here too long. I doubt I was even supposed to come here. I hope you think about everything I said. I hope you find God before it's too late." "Wait! But what are you doing!?" "Going back to where I belong." I closed the door, leaving her in God's hands. The only hands strong enough to break the chains she clung to so tightly.

I stepped off the subway onto the station in Ring Three, then the subway to Station Axwell. What I had habitually done for years. I climbed up the stairs and started down the street. When I reached the Merricks' house, I knocked on the door. Serah opened it. "Oh, hey, Elnora! What are you doing here?" "Where's Anthony?" "He's in the living room. Come on in." I went inside and followed Serah. "Look who's here, Anthony," she said cheerfully. Anthony smiled when he saw me. "Hey, Nora! Miss me, did you?" He walked over to me and tried to hug me. I pushed him away. "Don't you dare! Not after what you did!" He crossed his arms and smirked. "And what's that?" "You used me! You asked me all those questions last night to help Maddie! And now my family is going to die!" He laughed. "Family? When have those jerks ever been your family? They betrayed you, didn't they? Your own brother was the worst of them all. I'm the only person who really loves you." "No! *I* deceived *them*! And now I'm done! I should never have trusted you! I shouldn't have let myself believe that I could change you! We're done!" He frowned, obviously confused. "You're not being yourself, Nora. Let's go for a walk and talk about this. We'll figure things out." "No! For the first time since I've met you, I am being exactly myself! Exactly who God created me to be! And I'm done letting my feelings control me!" "Oh, is that so? We'll see how long that lasts. You'll come back. They always do." "I'm nothing like the other girls you've dated, Anthony. They let you use them and plead for more while you move on without a care. I'm not gonna let you keep your hooks in me! I'm breaking free! Because I'm not defined by you. I'm defined by what *God* says about me!" "Fine! Go ahead! I don't care!" I turned towards the door. His voice faltered. "Wait. No. Nora, you can't be serious?" I whipped around. "That's not my name! You know it's not! You've never used my name! It's *Elnora*! And I happen to like my name! I never want to hear that name again!" I slammed the door behind me, leaving him speechless. I stood outside their house, smiling wildly. What did the Bible say again? '*And whoever does not receive you nor listen to your words, as you leave that house or city, shake the dust off your feet.*' So that's what I did. I shook my feet and laughed. I laughed in a way that I hadn't in a long time. Not since before my parents died. I hadn't realized how much Anthony had bound me. And now I was free! Even so, there was more to do. There were more things to make right. I hurried down the street towards Harminny House. There was so much to do and so little time. But

I knew it could be done. Because God was finally holding the wheel.

CHAPTER THIRTEEN

I unlocked the hatch in the basement. "H-hey! Who's there?" I knew that voice! It was Amy. When she recognized me, her eyes narrowed. "You've got some guts coming back." I sighed. "I know, I'm sorry, Amy. I saw what happened, and I know I'm to blame. And I want to make things right. Will you please let me in?" She still didn't seem to trust me, but she said with a groan, "Fine. But you've got a lot to answer for." I sighed in relief and smiled. "Thanks, Amy." We climbed down into the sewers. "So, why'd you decide to come back after all that happened?" I sighed sadly. "I made a mistake. I followed my heart instead of God, and I'm here to repent of that." Amy laughed harshly. "A little late for that, don't you think?" "It's not too late to turn back. Not while there's breath in my lungs." "Is that so? Well, it might be too late for certain people. By the way, how is *that* your fault?" "Did you ever hear about me dating a guy in Ring Three?" "Oh, yeah, Matthew explained after you left. He assumed you went to live with him." I shook my head. "I didn't! You don't have to think *so* little of me. I went to live with my aunt. She's not a Christian, but she used to be. I thought I could change her mind. And I now realize that wasn't my responsibility. But I did not go to live with Anthony! However, I left so I could keep him because I believed I could show him the light. But again, that's not my job. Last night, he asked me a bunch of questions. I thought he was interested in my faith, but now I know that's not true. I've left both him and Aunt Elspeth." Amy unlocked the hatch into GIOR. "You've got a great story there. I just hope it's true, and you're not in cahoots with that government official." "I know there are so many reasons not to trust me. But I hope you will." "You can take it up with Kate. She's pretty upset about Jared's capture."

It was strange the feeling I got when I entered GIOR again. It felt light. I had no idea the darkness of Midas until I felt that. Though we were in a bomb shelter deep in the ground, it felt brighter than it did in the city. I wondered what made it feel this way. "Where's Kate?" Amy asked the guard. "She's in her apartment, but she's giving a speech in the cafeteria in a few minutes." "Thanks." I followed Amy into the cafeteria. Everyone had gathered around the stage. Kate approached the stage, holding Emory; Elizabeth and Elliot followed closely behind. She handed the toddler to Elizabeth, then stepped onto the small stage. She looked tired but determined. "Good afternoon, everyone. As you know, my husband Jared and a few others were captured last night. The Bible says, 'Fear not, for I am with you. Be not dismayed, for I am your God. I will uphold you with my righteous right hand.' So, we will not be afraid in this time. God is with us. We will instead pray, as the Bible says. Because when we pray, prison walls can shake. Chains can break. People are freed. So let us all pray that God will free our friends and family. And if he frees them by calling them into His heavenly kingdom, so be it. He is still good, and He still rescued them. Are you with me?" Shouts followed. "Then pray with me." Everyone bowed their heads. "Lord," Kate started. "We come before You in great need. The enemy has captured our friends and family. We know You are stronger than our enemy, and we believe You are with them. Please protect Jared, Matthew, Diana, Darcy, and Kendra. We ask that You protect them from any harm. We ask that You would save them. Whether that be by breaking down the prison walls or by calling them Home, we believe You will rescue them. We believe in all these things in Jesus' name, Amen." Tears fell down my face. I wanted faith like that. To see such dire circumstances and say, 'God, Your will be done.' Her husband could *die* tomorrow morning! And yet she has such faith. Faith that, even if he *died* that was God's plan. "I'm gonna go talk to Kate," I told Amy. I wove my way through the crowd until I reached the stage where she sat speaking to an older woman. "Thank you, Vanessa. You are very encouraging," she told her. The woman left, and Kate turned to me. She smiled kindly and hugged me. "Oh, praise God, you've come back! I've been praying for you every day since you left." I lost it then. "I'm so sorry, Kate! I shouldn't have left. And this is all my fault. I helped them capture them. I didn't realize at the time I was, but now I know I was. And I am *so* sorry! Will you please forgive me?" I pleaded, eyes to the ground, a torrent of tears spilling down my face. She lifted it. "Daughter, you already were." "I am?" She nodded. "Yes, you've repented. And God forgives when we repent. Now, why have you returned?" She motioned for me to sit. Tears poured down my face. "I've made a terrible mistake. I thought I would be okay. I thought I was doing what was right. I was wrong. I was following my heart, which is deceitful above *all* things, as the Bible says. I let my feelings guide me instead of the Holy Spirit. I decided my destiny was to change a boy I liked, but it only caused turmoil. And it's because of me that everyone has been captured. Last night, Anthony asked me a lot of questions. I thought he was interested in my faith, but I couldn't have been more wrong. He used me. And I'm sorry." I hung my head. Kate smiled. "Did you repent?" I nodded slowly. "Yes." "Are you still dating that boy?" "No." "Do you dedicate yourself to doing better?" I nodded and answered tearfully. "I do." "Then you are forgiven, daughter. By God, and by me." Kate hugged me. I sobbed with relief. She released me. "Now, there is more, isn't there?" I swallowed and nodded. "Yes." I paused. "I've come to rescue them." Kate blinked. "Rescue them?" "Yes, I know I don't deserve it, but I have a plan, and with the help of the Search and Rescue Team, we can save them." Kate's eyes brimmed with tears. "You are sure?" "Yes, more than anything!" She smiled. "Then you are the answer to my prayer. God is faithful." She turned to her children. "Elliot, go get Mr. Castrow." "Yes, Momma." The boy ran off.

Michael quickly came with Elliot. "What is it, Kate?" He noticed me and paled. He didn't look angry, though, like I thought he would. Was that *relief*? "You're back!" I nodded. "Yes, now could you get the team together as quickly as possible?" He nodded and pressed a button on a small black device on his belt. "They're on their way." "Good. Now, I know I don't deserve this." I brushed a loose strand of hair out of my face. "But I believe I need to lead this mission." He smiled. "Of course. Welcome back, Pip. See you in ten."

I returned to the apartment Matthew and I shared. My belongings remained undisturbed. Matthew's side showed signs of a rushed exit. I wondered what had brought him and Jared out in such a hurry. I changed into my black suit and bulletproof vest. I pinned my braid to the back of my head. And before I went out, I prayed, "God?" I took a deep breath. "You say You've chosen me for this moment. And I believe You. But I need You to help me. I'm not qualified for this at all. Please, guide me and give me wisdom." I left the apartment and went to the training facility.

Those remaining of the team were lined up in front of Michael: Cal, Ezra, Miriam, and Amy. I stood next to Amy. "Thank you for coming in on such short notice, team. We've got a big mission ahead of us. This isn't gonna be easy. I will be joining you for this, but not as the leader. For this mission, our leader will be Pip." I stepped forward. "You can't be serious, sir!" Amy exclaimed. "She abandoned us!" "And I'd advise you to, '*Keep your opinion to yourself!*' Pip is a part of the team and you will respect her as mission leader. And actually, since we're shorthanded, you get to be more than the pilot today." Her face lit up. "Really?" He nodded. "As long as you *respect* the mission leader."

She saluted. "Yes, sir." She looked fit to burst with excitement. "Now, listen up!" Michael stepped into line. My heart pounded. "Lord, give me strength," I whispered. "Thank you, everyone. I know I don't deserve to be here, and I know you probably haven't forgiven me yet. But I plead for you to work with me, at least for this mission. For the sake of our friends." I glanced at Cal. His face was very stern. He was still mad at me, of course. Why wouldn't he be? I'd hurt him the most out of everyone. I took a deep breath. My heart was still thundering like a drum. "They're being held in the Capitol building under close security. They know our games. They're going to be waiting for us. And I'm sure, with how she was on our last mission together, Miss Merrick will be there. They're counting on us coming. But here's the thing: they think we're desperate. But we're not. I know things are intense right now. I know we're all worried about them. But we have to hold firm. We have to think things through carefully. I'm talking to myself here, too. I know this is all crazy, and this all just looks like a suicide mission, but I need you all to trust me. So!" I tapped the tech board behind me. A blueprint of the Capitol building came up. I picked up the white pen and made a circle around the fifteenth floor. "This is where they'll be keeping them for questioning, no doubt by Miss Merrick and her colleagues. But that's what they want us to think. They're actually being kept *here*." I scrolled through the government buildings until I reached the science facility and tapped it. I circled underneath the building. "What are you talking about? There's no basement under the science facility. Look at the blueprint!" Ezra argued. "I heard it from an outside source." "Who? Your boyfriend?" Amy asked accusingly. "As a matter of fact, yes. Anthony did tell me this. They recently built it for science experiments outside of the public eye. That's where they'll be keeping them. And get this: it can be accessed through the sewers." I zoomed out the screen and tapped a different blueprint, one for the sewers. "There is an access point right here." I circled a specific hatch on the northeastern side of the sewer system. "This is right beneath the building, which means it's in the basement. It will be guarded. I doubt they'll be taking any chances, but not nearly as much as the Capitol building. We will escape through the sewer system as well, but we *must* avoid being followed. GIOR cannot be found. So, we will take them to my house, then lock them beneath the secret hatch. Then we may get just enough time to get out of their range so we can run to House Luke from there and reach GIOR. Any questions?" Ezra raised his hand. "Why should we believe you? Believe any of this? How do we know you're not working for them yourself?" I sighed. "I know it's hard, Ezra, but I really need you all to trust me for this. And I know I've done nothing to deserve that, but please, just for this mission." He thought for a moment, then nodded. "But only for Di, Bro, and Specs." "That's all I ask. Now, we'll be leaving in an hour, so we don't have much time to get prepared. This is going to be tough, but I know we can do this. Dismissed."

Amy and Ezra chatted quietly. Cal went to do target practice. But Michael and Miriam approached me. "That was a brilliantly thought-out plan, Pip. Kendra would be proud," Michael said. "Thank you, sir. I am grateful for all the blueprints." "I'm sure she'd be happy to hear that. She worked very hard on that database and making it easy to navigate." "How did she get captured?" "Diana received a note while she was at work yesterday. It was from her mother asking that she come home and bring one of her friends because she and her brother wanted to learn more about her faith. So, she and Kendra went, but it was a trap. What we now know is that many people received notes like that. Matthew received a note from you. He and Jared went to get you." "Oh." More of Maddie and Anthony's deceptions. "Dr. Bennet was just figured out by one of his colleagues while he was at work yesterday, and they reported him." "I'm sorry all this happened. It really is all my fault." Miriam hugged me. "Don't worry about that. I'm sure you didn't intend for this to happen." "Thank you." She smiled gently. "I'm glad you're back. And..." She paused and grinned. "I think Cal is, too." I blinked. "Cal?" I looked over to where he was shooting targets. "I don't think so. I hurt him the most when I left." "Yes, but he's never been one to hold something against someone. I've known him since he was little. Give him a chance. There's no harm in trying." I walked over to the shooting range. Cal shot another bullet. "Hi," I greeted him shyly. I put my hands behind my back, fidgeting with my fingers. "Hey." "You're good," I said. "My dad's an excellent teacher." I smiled and nodded. "He is." Silence... Well, I guess it was now or never. "I-I wanted to apologize for my behavior towards you. It was deceptive and wrong. And I'm sorry. I regret my actions." He didn't say anything for a moment. "You know you didn't have to go out with me if you liked someone else. You led me on when all you had to say was that you loved this guy. I would've understood." "I know. I just didn't want to upset you." "But you made everything worse by not telling me the truth." "I know. And I'm sorry." Neither of us said anything. The awkwardness was like a thick blanket of humidity. Finally, he asked, "Are you still dating him?" I shook my head. "No, it's over. We should've never been together in the first place. I know that now." "Good." He stuttered. "D-do you think that maybe there's a chance for me?" I smiled and nodded. "Yeah, I think there is." He smiled softly. "I just need some time to get my priorities in order again. And...I'll let you know." "Fine with me." He paused. "I really like you, Elnora." I felt my cheeks grow warm. "I know." He smiled, which made my heart flutter.

We all gathered at the hatch underneath the sewers of Ring One. "Everyone, ready?" I asked. They saluted. "Aye, aye, captain," Amy said. "Any final questions before we do this?" "Nope," Ezra replied eagerly. "Let's do this!" I laughed. "Great! Michael?" His brow rose in question. "Would you please pray before we go in?" He smiled and nodded. "Absolutely." We all bowed our heads and stood in a circle. Michael began, "Heavenly Father, we thank you for this chance to save our friends and family. We thank You for sending someone with the wisdom and knowledge to lead this mission. Please guide us and protect us. As Your word says, 'He who dwells in the shelter of the Most High will abide in the shadow of the Almighty. I will say to the Lord, 'My refuge and my fortress, my God, in whom I trust!' For it is He who delivers you from the snare of the trapper and from the deadly pestilence.' We pray this in Jesus' name, Amen." Michael looked at me as he loaded his gun and cocked it. "Ready when you are, Pip." I smiled confidently. "Cal, please open the hatch?" "On it." He climbed the ladder. "Quietly, please," I added. "Yes, ma'am." "Guns at the ready." I pressed the red button on the side of my gun to charge it up. Cal slid off the lid. We climbed up quietly. The lights were on, and white, smooth crates surrounded us. I tapped Ezra and signaled for him to follow me. We walked around the corner and came upon a lab. Several scientists were present; one individual was immobilized using a long, flat board and a white tube around their torso and arms. Kendra! "On my count. We stun all of them," I whispered. Ezra nodded. I held up three fingers, two, one. We rushed out, guns blazing, shooting tranqs into every lab coat in sight. Kendra struggled against her restraint. "There's a keycard in that one's pocket. It'll open it." The rest of the team came out. "Get the keycard, Mir." She dashed for the lead scientist on the floor. "Where are the others?" "Diana and Dr. Bennet are being held through there. Jared and Matthew are in the Capitol building." While Ezra and Cal hurried to release them, I stood in shock. "The Capitol building?" She nodded. "President Min wanted them close by. They're being held in his penthouse." "What?!" Mox exclaimed. "You're kidding!" She shook her head. "I wish I were. It would be so easy then, wouldn't it?" Miriam inserted the keycard. The restraints beeped and loosened. She removed them. Kendra shook out her arms. "Thanks." Michael hugged her like he hadn't seen her in years. "I'm so glad you're safe." She smiled. "I'm just glad you and Cal weren't captured, too." Cal and Ezra returned with Diana and Dr. Bennet. Both suffered bruises in many places. They were almost completely black and blue. "What happened?" I asked them. Diana laughed. "Nothing those geeks did. I just wouldn't come quietly, and neither would Doc." "I'll check you both out as soon as we get back," Miriam told them. "Good, then let's go. We gotta rescue Matthew and Jared," Diana said. "What?" Her eagerness surprised me. "Let's get back so I can get suited up. You're gonna need me." "But-no, Diana! You're hurt. Have you seen yourself?" "Don't need to. I know how I feel. Now, come on." I just stared. Some of the scientists stirred. "Come on, we gotta get out of here before they send for guards," Cal said. I nodded. "Right! Let's head out."

We returned to GIOR. After Miriam patched up Dr. Bennet and Diana, they joined us for a briefing on the next mission. "So, what's the plan, Pip?" Diana asked. I'd been thinking about what to do to rescue Jared and Matthew since we'd gotten back. I had a plan, but it would be risky. "As Kendra said, Jared and Matthew are being kept in the president's penthouse on the 100th floor of the Capitol building. This is going to be a really tough mission, but I only need four of you." "Four," Michael asked. "That's a risky number,

Elnora. What are you planning? Are you sure that's smart?" I swallowed. "I'm not certain. But I have a plan, and I think it's a good plan. And for it, we need as few numbers as possible." "And who do you want?" "Cal, Diana, Amy, and Doc. Everyone else is dismissed." The rest of them saluted and left. "What's the plan, Pip?" Diana asked. I circled the 100th floor. "I'm sure you know already, but the penthouse is going to be under lockdown, especially with prisoners being held there. But I have a plan, and as I've said, it requires very few people. Doc is going to be the owner of a new company, and Cal will be his nephew who is learning about business. You two will ask to see the president about an investment. You won't see anyone else. If they send you someone, keep asking for him. Meanwhile, Diana, Amy, and I will fly to the research building and zipline to the Capitol building and climb through the ventilation to the penthouse. We'll communicate through earpieces, and as soon as we're escaping with Jared and Matthew, you can conclude the meeting. Then we all head home." No one said anything. "You were right when you said it would be risky," Cal finally said, scratching the back of his head. "But I like it," Diana said with a smirk. "Let's do this!" I smiled. It was looking good. But worry still filled my mind. If we failed, we could all die, and so would Matthew and Jared. Oh, God, please help us!

CHAPTER FOURTEEN

"Are you sure about this, Pip?" Amy asked as we landed on the research building. "If we fail-" "I know, Mox. But we have no other options. It's this or Matthew and Jared die." She nodded in understanding. Diana took a winch from her belt and pulled the trigger. The hook fastened to the top of the Capitol building. She pulled out some handlebars and hooked them onto the line. "Ready whenever you are, captain." She saluted. "Thanks, Di." I grabbed onto the handlebars and kicked off. My heart pounded. If my hands slipped, I would plummet into the streets. Oh, dear Lord, don't let me fall! I reached the top of the Capitol building and gasped in relief. I sent the handlebars back to the other two and cocked my gun in case someone heard us. Thankfully, no one had. Once all three of us were on the roof, I pressed the button on my earpiece. "We've reached the roof. Any updates, Doc?" His smooth, deep voice came through in reply. "They've taken us to the president's office. He'll be meeting us soon." "Great. We'll head in." Diana opened the vent. I angled myself in carefully, grateful for no big drop. "Okay, we're good. Come on." Diana and Amy climbed in. We crept carefully and noiselessly through the steel tube until I reached the first vent in the ceiling. I looked through, listening carefully. I heard and saw nothing. "Screwdriver?"

Diana handed one to me. I removed the screws and carefully opened the vent to avoid making noise and alerting people to our presence. I dropped in. The penthouse was gorgeous. I'd never seen a place so richly decorated and pristinely clean. All the furniture was white, except for the tables, which were made of light-colored wood. "Do you know where they could be kept?" "No, I just know they're being kept here. I doubt they'll be in plain sight, though." I agreed. "Come on, let's search the place." I scanned the living room and tapped the walls for any sign of a hidden room. Nothing. I walked into the bedroom. How strange it felt to be in the president's bedroom. Such a personal place of someone I'd only seen from afar, not to mention the murderer of my parents. I looked around. The bed was on a carpeted platform. Huh? I'd seen that kind of thing before, but part of me wondered if perhaps it was a secret hiding place. I tried to lift the platform. It gave slightly, but it was really heavy. "Di, Mox, come help me with this!" They ran in. Diana hooked a spray can back on to her belt. "This lifts up," I told them. "But it's really heavy. I need your help." Diana and I took a corner, and Amy took the middle. "Three, two, one. Lift!" The platform lifted and fit perfectly lined up with the wall and now revealed was a large steel hatch. "Bingo," Diana said. I tried to open it, but it wouldn't budge. That's when I noticed the key card slot. "We need a key card." She groaned and wiped her face. "Of course we do." I stood up. "Well, maybe it's in here somewhere." She shook her head. "Everything is on high authority access here. The president would carry his keycard with him. We need to find someone who has the same access level." "What about that interrogator girl?" Amy asked. "Maddie?" "Yeah. Do you think she'd have this kind of access?" "Perhaps. But we can't exactly depend on speculation here. We don't have time." "Well, maybe he has a spare?" "He could. Let's look." We ravaged through his drawers. Nothing. "He probably has an office up here. Let's check that out."

His office was equally nice, but much less decorated compared to the rest of the penthouse. There was a keycard right on his desk! I picked it up. "Found it!" We hurried back to the bedroom. I swiped the card, and the door unlocked. I opened it and gasped in surprise. Matthew and Jared! Crammed into a deep, dark, small space, there was no room between them. Strips of fabric gagged them. They exclaimed in joy. Diana and I pulled them out. I untied Matthew's gag and used the keycard to unlock their restraints. "Oh, Matthew!" I felt tears prick my eyes. He was beaten and bruised, but I'd never been more glad to see him. I hugged him. "I'm so glad you're okay." He held me close. "You came back?" I nodded. "I couldn't just sit by and watch the government kill my brother." Cal's voice blared over my earpiece. "You guys gotta get outta there! They got an alert of a security breach! They're coming!" I pressed the button. "Are you and Doc okay?" "Yeah, we're on our way out of the building now." "Great. We've got them, so we're leaving." I looked at the girls. "They got an alert. We have to go." I helped Matthew up. "Can you walk?" He nodded. "How about you, Jared?" Diana tried to help him stand, but he lost his footing and fell. He groaned. "Sorry." "Can you carry him, Di?" She tried to lift him. "Not on my own." I helped her hold Jared up. "Mox, you go get the transport." She nodded and ran out. "With Jared's condition, we'll have to go out the fire exit. It's out in the hall." Diana sighed. I turned to my brother and handed him my gun. "Can you cover us?" He took it and nodded. "Alright, let's go." Matthew opened the door and shot the gun, then urged us out. We hurried as much as we could, with Jared on our backs. Matthew shot a few more times. I used the keycard to open the fire exit. We hurried up the stairs. "Come on, Matthew!" He followed behind us, gun at the ready. We reached the top. Amy was waiting with the helicopter. Diana stood on the edge of the passenger area as we carefully transferred Jared to the helicopter. Matthew and I stepped on, and we flew away.

"We did it!" Amy exclaimed over the intercom. "We did it!" I gasped, laughing like a maniac. "We really did it!" Diana laughed. "Nice job, Captain." I hugged Matthew. "I'm so sorry I left." "It's okay." "It's over between me and Anthony." "I'm sorry." "Don't be. I ended it. And I'm glad I did." "That's good." I turned to Jared. He was propped up against the wall. "I'm so sorry, Jared." "It's okay, Elnora. I'm just so relieved you returned. Kate and I have been praying for you ever since you left." I hugged him. "Thank you." Diana was laughing smugly about something. "What's so funny?" Matthew asked. She pulled a spray can from her belt. "Oh, I just left the president a little message."

"Sir, the prisoners are gone." President Xao Min groaned and tightened his fists, then took a deep breath. "Pull up security camera footage. I want to see how they did it, so we can make sure it doesn't happen again." "Yes, sir." "And Nichols?" The government official turned back to him. "Yes, sir?" "It *won't* happen again." He swallowed. "Yes, sir." He left. The young interrogator who had captured the Christians approached him. "Sir, there's something you should see." She led him to his office. On the wall behind his desk, in blood red paint that was still dripping, was, "AND HE WILL CRUSH THE SERPENT'S HEAD."

EPILOGUE

It's been six months since the execution of our parents. So much has happened. So much has changed. After we rescued everyone, the president put the city on lockdown for a week. Authorities canceled all incoming and outgoing flights until further notice. Midas is under a state of emergency. But that hasn't stopped us. We're still growing, still building, still saving people. Matthew and I are now interns under the Brenwoods. We also learn a lot from the Castrows. Cal and I are good friends. But that's all. For now. I haven't seen Jeffrey in a while. I miss him, and I pray for him. But I believe he's okay. And I hope to see him show up to a teaching some evening. I heard from Anthony once. He left me a note at Harminny House asking me to come back, that what happened was just a heat-of-the-moment thing, and he regretted what was said. But I wasn't tempted for a moment. I won't ever go back. It's hard to believe how much has happened. And there's still more to come, but I'm not afraid. God is with us every step of the way. I know without a shadow of a doubt that He chose me for this time, so He will help me. But that doesn't mean I don't need other people. I tried to do it on my own. To save the world by myself. And I'll never do it again. The fact is, we're all chosen. God has decided we're exactly what the world needs for our time. If only we all realized that. How much braver would we be? How much bolder? How many lives could be saved? How many people would be set free? We so easily forget about how precious we are. How intentionally made we are. I know that we live in a fallen world where bad things happen, even to good people. But maybe, with the truth instilled in us, we could make things better. We could be heroes. Not superheroes with capes or masks that fly around saving the world from supervillains. No. The only hero that super is the One who saved us. But He chose to save us. He chose me. He chose Matthew. He chose everyone at GIOR. He even chose Maddie and Anthony. If they could one day choose to see that. And I pray that they will, even though they tried to stop us. But there's more to be done. Things are only going to get harder for us. But we'll never stop fighting. Not as long as there's breath in our lungs. Until the day comes when He'll make everything new, we have a mission. A mission that includes everyone who calls on His Name. A mission to show everyone the God who chose them. And we all have a part to play. Because we are all chosen.

END OF BOOK ONE

ACKNOWLEDGMENTS

First of all, I'd like to thank you, reader, for picking this book up and giving it a chance. This book is truly my heart for the world, and I hope and pray that you have been inspired by it. I've been writing dedicatedly for four years, and it's so surreal that I'm actually a published author now.

A huge thanks to my beta readers: Savannah, Anabelle, and my dear sister, Raphaella. You fell in love with this story in its messiest stage, and I can't thank you enough for all the feedback and support you've given me. Without it, Chosen would not be what it is today.

I'd also like to thank my boyfriend Tyler, who has spent much time reading my work and listening to me ramble about it for hours on end as I figure things out in my head. Thank you for being my cheerleader and believing in me when I didn't even believe in myself.

Thank you to my wonderful parents who have supported me in pursuit of this and helped me in any way possible to bring me closer to my dreams. I couldn't ask for better parents. Your dedication to your own dreams inspires me every day and makes me believe that I can do it too.

And finally, because it's the biggest one, I thank God, for saving me and loving me so much more than I can possibly comprehend. The only reason Chosen was born was through Your leading and guiding my words as I wrote, and I thank You for choosing me to write it. I will never deserve it.

AUTHOR'S NOTE

If after reading this you want to know the God who chose you, I encourage you to pursue that call. I could write a whole book of all the things I've seen and experienced myself that proves the faithfulness and goodness of our Creator, but as John 21:25 says: *"Now there are also many other things that Jesus did. Were every one of them to be written, I suppose that the world itself could not contain the books that would be written."* Even if you've answered the call before, sometimes we stray, sometimes the worries of this life wears us out, sometimes we just don't understand what that really means, I encourage you to seek the Father. He is everything you could possibly need or want. But He wants you to choose Him. And you may feel that you are not deserving of that unconditional love like Aunt Elspeth, maybe you feel you've done too much to accept that grace. But God doesn't care who you are or what you have done. Your very existence means He chose you. And He chose you for a reason. You have something that no one else does, something that can change the world. Just let yourself fall into His arms and feel the great love that He has for you.

The Bible says in Romans 10:9-11: *"Because, if you confess with your mouth that Jesus is Lord and believe in your that God raised Him from the dead, you will be saved. For with the heart one believes and is justified, and with the mouth one confesses and is saved. For the Scripture says, 'Everyone who believes in Him will not be put to shame.'"* It's not complicated or difficult. Just let go and let yourself be loved.

ABOUT THE AUTHOR

Annaliese is a storyteller by nature. Growing up inspired by heroines like Anne Shirley, Katniss Everdeen, and Jo March, she desires to inspire others with Biblical truths and the love of Christ. Her debut novel, Chosen, is a call to be courageous in a world prone to fear and complacency. A proud homeschool graduate, she  spends her days reading, writing, and thriving on her family's sheep farm.

Connect on Goodreads:

https://www.goodreads.com/user/show/185072264-annaliese-layaw

Printed in Dunstable, United Kingdom